SCANDAL ROCKS SIOUX FALLS!

Yeeeoww! Just when we were going through a dry spell of sordid Sioux Falls couplings to report, do we have a scoop for you....

Our trusted paparazzi confirm that there was a passionate undertone when sexy Aussie Max Fortune shot daggers at widowed heiress Diana Fielding-Young from across the room during Case Fortune's engagement soiree. The commanding cattle baron from Down Under is supposedly in town to get his new horse-breeding venture off the ground, but perhaps he's really here to make his former lover suffer for trampling on his overinflated ego.

Twelve years prior, our lovelorn couple steamed up the sheets all summer long in Australia. But it was splitsville for those two when Ms. Fielding-Young deserted him—right before he dropped down on his knee to propose, no less!—to become the trophy wife of a much older man. Well, she sure ain't a grieving widow these days. She still has it bad for her former lover, who isn't exactly rebuffing her.

But does trouble loom on the horizon? Her late hubby's money grubbing sons are trying to wrestle away her inheritance and—catch this!—claim she was prone to sleazy extramarital affairs. Be sure to catch our next edition that will be chock-full of more nefarious details.

Dear Reader,

Welcome back to the world of DAKOTA FORTUNES, the continuing saga of the Fortune family. In *Back in Fortune's Bed,* author Bronwyn Jameson weaves the fabulously enticing tale of Australian Max Fortune and the woman he's bound and determined to have back in his bedroom.

Why would a woman with any sense have run away from a catch like Max? Diana had her reasons…and they are pretty good ones. But she'll have a heck of a time convincing Max of them, provided he'll let her get a word in. He's bent on revenge and she has little choice but to succumb.

I hope you enjoy this latest installment of the DAKOTA FORTUNES series and that you'll join us next month when Charlene Sands brings us Eliza's story in *Fortune's Vengeful Groom.* Seems this eldest Fortune daughter has been keeping a big secret from her own family.

Happy reading,

Melissa Jeglinski

Melissa Jeglinski
Senior Editor
Silhouette Books

Please address questions and book requests to:
Silhouette Reader Service
U.S.: 3010 Walden Ave., P.O. Box 1325, Buffalo, NY 14269
Canadian: P.O. Box 609, Fort Erie, Ont. L2A 5X3

BRONWYN JAMESON

BACK IN FORTUNE'S BED

Silhouette® Desire

Published by Silhouette Books

America's Publisher of Contemporary Romance

For my research helpers, Marilyn, Heather, Laurie, Lisa,
Sarah. I couldn't have written this one without your help.
Thank you.

Special thanks and acknowledgment are given
to Bronwyn Jameson for her contribution to
DAKOTA FORTUNES miniseries.

 **SILHOUETTE BOOKS**

ISBN-13: 978-0-373-76777-9
ISBN-10:   0-373-76777-3

BACK IN FORTUNE'S BED

Visit Silhouette Books at www.eHarlequin.com

Printed in U.S.A.

BRONWYN JAMESON

spent much of her childhood with her head buried in a book. As a teenager, she discovered romance novels, and it was only a matter of time before she turned her love of reading them into a love of writing them. Bronwyn shares an idyllic piece of the Australian farming heartland with her husband and three sons, a thousand sheep, a dozen horses, assorted wildlife and one kelpie dog. She still chooses to spend her limited downtime with a good book. Bronwyn loves to hear from readers. Write to her at bronwyn@bronwynjameson.com.

THE DAKOTA FORTUNES

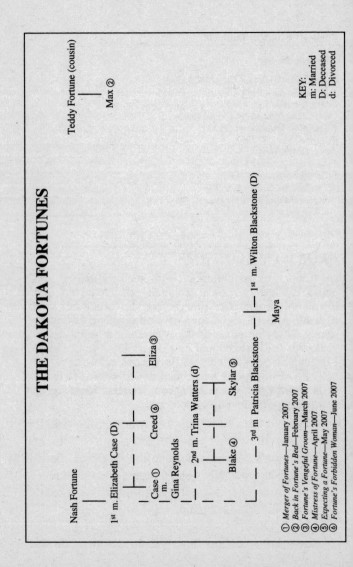

Nash Fortune

1st m. Elizabeth Case (D)

Teddy Fortune (cousin)

Max ②

Case ①
m.
Gina Reynolds

Creed ⑥

Eliza ③

2nd m. Trina Watters (d)

Blake ④

Skylar ⑤

3rd m Patricia Blackstone — — 1st m. Wilton Blackstone (D)

Maya

① *Merger of Fortunes*—January 2007
② *Back in Fortune's Bed*—February 2007
③ *Fortune's Vengeful Groom*—March 2007
④ *Mistress of Fortune*—April 2007
⑤ *Expecting a Fortune*—May 2007
⑥ *Fortune's Forbidden Woman*—June 2007

KEY:
m: Married
D: Deceased
d: Divorced

Prologue

"It *is* her."

Max Fortune's muttered words went unheard, swallowed by the chatter that rose and fell in waves around him. Not that Max noticed. His focus remained riveted on the woman who'd captured his attention the instant he walked into the party at his Dakota cousins' grand estate home.

There'd been something about her posture and the way she tilted her head to listen intently to her companion's conversation that had jangled at deeply buried memories. When she'd turned enough to reveal her face in profile, kick-gut recognition had shocked the words loose from his mind.

It *was* Diana Fielding.

Ten years older but there was no mistaking the distinctive dip in her nose or the low-set eyebrows that gave her face a somberness at odds with her smile. There was no mistaking that high-octane smile, either, or the startling contrast between her milky skin and night-dark hair. Still long, he presumed, although tonight she wore it up, drawing attention to the smooth line of her throat.

There'd been a time when Max had kissed every inch of that long, slender column...when he'd kissed every inch of her long, slender body.

What the hell was that body doing in South Dakota?

Max had only arrived himself that afternoon. Despite the lengthy series of flights from his home in Australia via New Zealand and L.A., he'd accepted his hosts' party invitation without hesitation. It provided the perfect opportunity to meet all of Nash Fortune's family—Case, Creed, Eliza, Blake and Skylar, his cousins several-times-removed—in the one place. Max appreciated that kind of efficiency. In fact, he'd accepted Nash and his wife Patricia's invitation to base this business trip here because Sioux Falls provided efficient access to all the horse breeding farms he aimed to visit.

Visiting with this branch of his extended family for the first time was an added bonus.

Revisiting the worst moment in his life—now that was an add-on he could do without.

"What's up, mate? You look like you've seen a ghost."

Max turned to find Zack Manning, his New Zealand based friend, business partner and traveling companion, eyeing him closely. "Not a ghost," he said with a casual shrug that belied the tension in his gut. "Just a woman I thought I knew once."

His friend's breath whistled out between his teeth as he studied the object of Max's distraction. "Y'know, I think you'd remember meeting *her.*"

No kidding.

"Looks European," Zack decided. "Like a Russian princess."

She wasn't, although speech lessons had edged her voice with an accent as regal as her show-biz-royalty blood. She'd hated him drawing attention to that; she'd determinedly played it down...until he'd mentioned how it turned him on. Then she'd employed it with impressive effect.

"Looks as though you're about to make the princess's acquaintance," Zack said.

Everything inside him twanged like high tensile wire as his gaze swung across the room. There, at Diana Fielding's side, his cousin Eliza was trying to catch his attention. Suddenly her presence here made sense. She was visiting with Eliza—the two of them had been friends at college. He should have remembered the connection since it had led, indirectly, to their meeting.

Eliza waved her hand harder and, curse it, he couldn't ignore that summons. Or the elbow his friend used to nudge him into motion. "Geez, Fortune. I've never known you so reluctant to meet a beautiful woman."

"I'm not here to meet women."

"A good thing," Zack quipped, "given that scowl you're wearing would send 'em screaming from the room."

In deference to his hosts and their guests, Max made

an effort to wipe his mind and his expression clear of dark memories. Lord knew he'd had enough practice over the years.

Ten years, seven months, two weeks, to be precise.

When Eliza caught his hand and pulled him into the small group, he managed a stiff smile. "You know Case," she said, indicating the eldest of her brothers, whom he'd met that afternoon. "This is his date, Gina Reynolds. And this is Diana Young."

Not Diana Fielding. Not any more.

"Hello, Max."

His smile faded. He remembered the first time they'd met and the same warm I-*am*-pleased-to-meet-you look in her grey-green eyes as they looked into his. And he remembered the last time he'd seen her, the day he traveled to New York with a diamond ring in his pocket.

The day he'd stood undetected in the shadows watching her walk through a petal-strewn garden to marry another man.

"Diana…Young, is it?"

He saw the confusion in her eyes, then the slight recoil as she absorbed the cool cut of his question.

But that was nothing compared to the knife of betrayal she'd driven into him ten years before. At the time he'd thought that wound had pierced his heart. Later he'd decided it was only damage to his pride, his male ego, his crushed plans. The scar shouldn't still hurt. It wouldn't, he declared with absolute conviction, if this meeting hadn't come as such a god-sudden out-of-the-blue shock.

Turning his gaze to Eliza and Case and Gina, he

detected a weight of curiosity in their silence and knew
he couldn't play nice for the sake of etiquette. He couldn't
fake small talk. And he was in no mood to explain his
previous relationship with Diana Fielding Young.

"If you'll excuse me, I need to pay my respects to
Patricia and Nash. I haven't caught up with them yet."
He knew his words sounded stiff, but he managed a
smile for Case's date. "Nice to meet you, Gina."

He had nothing to say to Diana. Nothing he could say
in this polite company. He nodded curtly and walked away.

One

Over the past two weeks Diana had done upset, disappointed, annoyed, indignant and a dozen other emotions too confusing and complex and maddening to label. Right now, walking through the breezeway in Skylar Fortune's barn, she would have chosen any one of them over her current state of jittery, heart-jumping nerves.

Fitting, she supposed, since Sky's stables were filled with similarly high-strung thoroughbreds.

Not that she could blame her current state on either the location or her semi-fear of horses. Nor could she blame the purpose of her early morning visit to the Fortune estate, which was to shoot her first professional we-pay-you photos. Ever. That caused her nerves to hum with barely suppressed excitement not to wail with trepidation.

The wailing and the jittering were all down to one thing.

Here, in the stables that were his domain, she risked running into Max Fortune again.

She hated that his snub at Case's party had tied her in knots for the two weeks since. Had he not recognized her? Did he not remember her? Or had he left so abruptly after their short exchange because he didn't want to acknowledge their history?

Eventually she'd admonished herself for wasting too much emotional energy on an old love affair. After three years of widowhood she'd finally found her feet. Since moving to Sioux Falls she'd lucked upon an occupation she loved and had recently taken up a position at her mentor's studio/gallery.

The last thing she needed was a force of nature like Max Fortune messing with her newly discovered contentment.

For the duration of the twenty-mile drive from Sioux Falls to the Fortune estate, she'd reprised that lecture. Today was crucial to her aspirations. She needed to remain focused and professional.

But all the self-talk in the world didn't stop her heart from leaping into her throat when she heard the crunch of hooves on aged brick cobblestones. Pivoting on her heels, she looked back over her shoulder at the approaching horse being led by…Skylar.

Thank you, God.

She released a long breath and smiled as the youngest of Nash Fortune's five children came to an abrupt halt, her brows knit in a frown. "Diana. You're here. Already."

"I know I'm a little early." On her first job she'd thought that infinitely better than tardiness. "I can wait until you're ready. There's no rush."

"No, it's okay. I'm pretty sure Max has your model all gussied up and ready for the camera."

The impatient horse at Sky's side stamped its feet in unison with the lurch of Diana's heart. She took a half-step back from its large feet, just to be on the safe side. "Max?"

"Max Fortune. Our Aussie cousin. Didn't you meet him at Case's party?" Without waiting for an answer, Sky hurried on. "Not to worry, you'll meet him now. Max and his friend Zack Manning are starting up a stud farm back home and they're over here inspecting the set-ups and buying stock. Your subject is one of Max's first acquisitions and she's a real beauty. He bought her in Kentucky last week."

"Do you mean that this job is shooting *Max Fortune's* horse?"

As soon as the words left her mouth, Diana wished them back. Not the question itself—that was perfectly valid since Sky had made the booking without one mention of a third party—but her horror-struck tone.

Sky's frown deepened. "I didn't realize that would be a problem."

"Oh, no, it's not a problem," Diana lied.

"Really? Because you said poor Max's name as if you'd just as soon shoot him. And I don't mean with your camera!"

Oh, joy. That's exactly what she'd feared. The perfect nonprofessional start when Sky had paid her a huge compliment by booking her instead of an equine specialist.

"Would you prefer if I got someone else?"

"Oh, no, that's not necessary," Diana said quickly. She'd come here as a photographer, not as a woman bruised by a past breakup or a recent snub. She could do this. She could be polite, businesslike, friendly even. "I'm here to shoot whatever you point me at…and only with my camera."

"Sure?"

Diana smiled with what she hoped passed for cheerful assurance while her chest tightened with un-cheerful apprehension. "Absolutely. Now, where will I find your Aussie cousin?"

Following Sky's directions, Diana turned from the wide central breezeway into one of two wings added to the original barn when Sky expanded her horse breeding enterprise. *Barn* hardly described the giant U-shaped dwelling now. The place was five star accommodation, meticulously clean and toasty warm despite the frigid winter's morning outside.

Diana dispensed with her gloves and loosened the scarf she'd wrapped around her neck. So she'd be ready to start work. And because her fluttery fingers needed something further to do, she hitched her camera bag more securely on her shoulder and increased her pace to a confident stride.

One thing she'd learned from her stage-star mother was how to exude presence, even when her insides were trembling up a storm.

At the second to last stable, she stopped and gathered her well-learned poise. Over the high Dutch door all she could see was the tail end of a large horse. The Kentucky beauty, she presumed, although not from her best angle.

Trepidation caused her heart to drum harder as she approached the door. For a second she thought the animal was unattended but then she heard his voice. Too low to make out the words, but she recognized the deep crooning tone.

Unfortunately her hormones recognized it, too, not from the days spent at his outback stables but from the nights spent in his bed. They stretched and yawned and shimmied to life before she could do a dashed thing to control their recollections.

This was not the response she needed right now, not when the rustling of straw announced him moving around beyond the horse's substantial frame.

She took a rapid step backward and drew a deep breath just as he came into view, looking exactly like the Max she'd tried so hard, for so long, to forget.

His suede western jacket and wide-brimmed hat were pure cowboy, although that label had amused the heck out of him whenever she'd used it. *Cattleman* was the term they used in Australia. And although Max worked his family's outback cattle ranches, he spent equal time running the business side of the operation from behind an office desk.

Or he had.

Past tense, Diana reminded herself. Max Fortune might still wear his tan Akubra low to shade his deep green eyes. He might still wear his hair long enough to curl beneath the broad brim of that trademark hat, but a lot can change in ten years.

A lot *had* changed, but not her body's elemental response to the man.

Everything tightened and warmed and raced as she watched one large hand smooth a path over the horse's gleaming rump. "You'll do just fine, sweetheart," he murmured, his voice as languid as that slow-moving hand.

Diana felt a shivery pang in the pit of her stomach, a reaction and an anticipation as he started to turn toward the stable door. She caught the edge of his easy grin and her stomach went into free-fall.

This wasn't the grim stranger from the party but the lover she remembered, quick to smile, to tease, to laugh.

Then he caught sight of her and the smile faded from his mouth and his eyes, leaving his expression as cold as a Dakota February dawn.

Diana resisted the urge to rub at her arms or rewrap her scarf. She searched for the right opening line but all she could find was the same simple greeting as two weeks earlier at the party. "Hello, Max."

"Diana."

No *hello,* just her name spoken in a tone as flat and dry as the outback plains of his home.

That short greeting did, however, answer her earlier unspoken question. He recognized her all right, which meant she hadn't imagined his snub at the party. She couldn't pretend that the knowledge didn't hurt, but today he was her client. She had to forget their past encounters, both recent and distant, and focus on the job.

"Is this the mare you want photographed?" she asked.

"*You're* the horse photographer?"

She bit back the instant response—*is that so hard to believe?*—because the answer was written all over his face. Way back when he'd teased her about her degree in arts and the classics, about her society-girl lifestyle and lack of a work résumé of any description. This was her opportunity to show that she could do something practical, and that she could do it well.

"That is what I'm here for," she said crisply, reaching for the clip on her camera bag.

"Is it?"

Alerted by the skepticism in his tone, she looked up and found him eyeing her, head to toe and back again. "Why else would I be here?" she asked.

"Beats me. From what I remember, horses scare the living daylights out of you."

"That was a long time ago, Max. I'm not that girl any more."

Something shifted in his expression, and Diana stiffened in expectation of what he might say about the past and the hours he'd spent coaxing the horse-shy New Yorker into the saddle on one of his Australian stock horses.

But perhaps all she'd seen was a wall going up, because he said nothing about the past, returning instead to their present situation.

"You don't look like you've come here to work with horses," he pointed out. "You're wearing a skirt."

A frown pinched her brows together as she glanced down at her clothes. Had she broken an unwritten dress code for equine photographers? Yes, she wore a skirt but it was a conservative A-line, teamed with a cable-knit sweater and practical low-heeled boots. The outfit would take her from this job to a charity committee meeting Eliza had roped her into, without needing to go home to change.

"I understood Sky booked me," she said, cool, polite, restrained, "to take a simple portrait of a horse. She didn't mention it was your horse. Believe me, I am as surprised as you about that! But I am here to do that job and if that requires me to get down and dirty for artistic angles or special effects, just say the word. I'm sure Sky will loan me some jeans."

Although his jaw flexed, he remained blessedly silent. Diana decided to take that as a positive sign, but only because this job meant too much to blithely toss it away. Establishing herself as a photographer was the first goal she'd been passionate about in a long, long while. There was a certain cruel irony in the fact that her start involved working with the last object of her total passion. But she wouldn't allow that joke-of-fate to drive her away. She might have set out this morning with the aim of proving herself to herself, but in the last few minutes it had become equally important to prove herself to Max.

With a brisk and businesslike nod of her head, she indicated the horse now prowling the stable at his back. "So, this is the job?"

"Yes."

Diana met his eyes and there, behind the flat, guarded admission, she read acceptance—albeit reluctant—of her role. Silently she breathed a sigh of relief. "Then let's talk about the photos you require."

"What do you suggest?" he asked after a measured pause. "You're the expert."

It was a test, she knew, since Max Fortune always knew exactly what he wanted. He'd told her as much the night they met. The night he decided he wanted her in his bed.

He'd been the expert then, but today it was her turn.

Nerves flapped vulture-sized wings in her stomach as she considered the challenge he'd set. She *had* photographed horses once—Sky's horses, as it happened. That had been a class assignment back before Christmas and she'd spent long hours alternatively perched on a railing fence and prone in the frozen meadow capturing the vibrant spirit, the athleticism, and the individual personalities of a group of colts in a field beyond Sky's barn.

The results had impressed her teacher so much that he'd included them in a winter exhibition in his gallery and then offered her a job there. They'd impressed Sky so much that she'd offered her this job.

Which left one person still to impress....

He was leaning on the half-door, watching her watch his horse. That silent observation fed more adrenaline into her system and she had to fight a momentary attack of *who-am-I-fooling* panic. Throwing up her breakfast would not look expert, capable or professional.

Forcing her focus to the horse as it paced the roomy stable, she framed a series of shots through an imaginary viewfinder. What she saw settled and excited her nerves in equal measures. Could she capture that ripple of muscles beneath the horse's burnished copper coat? Could she depict all that latent power in a single flat dimension?

"I'll have to take her moving," she decided, "in order to do her justice."

"Not a portrait?"

"That would be too static, don't you think?" He looked dubious, but the longer Diana watched the animal's graceful stride, the more confident she became in her first instinctive call. She tried another angle. "I gather she's a racehorse?"

"A retired one."

"Was she a fast one?"

"Fast and strong," he supplied, and the softened note of respect in his voice drew Diana's gaze back to his profile. Still the same square jaw that framed his face in steely strength.

Or, when he wanted his own way, in stubborn determination.

But the years had sculpted change in the hollowed planes beneath his cheekbones, in the fretted lines radiating from the corners of his narrowed gaze, in the straight set of his unsmiling mouth.

Diana longed to ask what had turned him so stern and disapproving, and why he was directing that acrimony toward her. But in talking about his horse she sensed the first easing in the tension between them and she wanted to prolong that mood. It wasn't exactly harmonious but it was a start.

"I would like to depict her as that fast, strong athlete you described. In motion. With the sun on her coat." She paused, watching his face, trying to gauge his reaction. "That's what I see when I look at her, but you're the client."

"And the client is always right?"

"No, but the client pays the bill so he always has the final say."

As if she wanted the final word, the horse extended her neck over the door and whinnied softly. Aware of Max's watchfulness, of being under his judgment, she forced herself to hold her ground. The horse seemed friendly enough. It was sniffing at her hair. No teeth were visible, which had to be a good thing. Diana took a steadying breath.

"Hello," she said softly, and was pleased that her voice didn't betray her horse-getting-far-too-close jeebies. "What is your name, beautiful?"

Max might have cleared his throat. Or it could have been a throaty horse noise from a neighboring stable. Diana lifted a hand—it hardly shook at all—and stroked the horse's face. A brass plate attached to the leather halter she wore was engraved with a single word.

"Bootylicious," she read. Brows lifted in surprise and amusement, she turned to Max. "Is that her name?"

"Don't blame me." He held up both hands defensively. "The name came with her."

And it was *so* not a name he would have chosen. Diana couldn't help smiling. "I think it is a very fitting name. Unique and distinctive," she said, pleased that the tension had eased enough that she *could* joke and smile without it feeling like her face might split with the effort. "Perfect for a foundation mare for your new stud farm," she continued, tongue-in-cheek. "You could name all her offspring Booty-*something*."

He shot her a disgusted look. "Luckily she's not part of the new operation."

"She's not? From what Sky said, I thought you and Zack were over here buying breeding stock."

"We are." He shifted his position, allowing the bootylicious one room to move off, before he leaned back against the door. Almost relaxed, Diana noted, with rich satisfaction. And finally he'd stopped glowering. "This mare was a champion miler but she's got too much sprinter's blood in her pedigree."

"Is that a bad thing?"

"Not for some studs, but we're looking to breed champion stayers...for long distance races," he clarified, when she looked askance. "This one's bloodlines don't fit the bill."

"But you bought her anyway?"

"A gift for my parents. I'm leaving her here with Sky until she's safely in foal. That's why I want the photos, to send them in lieu of the real thing."

"Easier to gift wrap."

"Much," he agreed, and a hint of the lopsided grin she loved lurked around the corners of his mouth.

Loved? Diana gave herself a quick mental shake. What they'd shared was not love, no matter what she'd thought during those blissful months. Mention of his parents whom she had never met acted as the perfect reminder.

"How is your family?" she asked out of politeness.

"They're all well."

"And you, Max?" Not out of politeness, but because she couldn't help herself. She had to know. "How have you been?"

"Fine."

On the surface it sounded liked a stock answer, the kind you pay no heed to. But all traces of that near-smile had vanished from his face and, as he pushed off the door and started toward the horse, Diana detected a stiffening in his posture.

Alarm fluttered in her chest. "Are you?" she asked, before she could think better of it.

"Why would you assume otherwise?"

"Because you seem so different, so—" she let her hands rise and fall as she struggled to describe the vibes he'd been giving off "—uptight."

"You said you're not the same person. Same goes."

Okay, but now he sounded downright hostile and Diana couldn't let it go. Not now that she'd started. "We've both changed, as people tend to do, but at Case's party you were unfriendly to the point of rudeness. I thought you might have been too travel-lagged to recognize me, or that you simply may not have remembered. But that's not the problem, is it?"

He clipped a lead rope onto the horse's halter before he turned. The hat shaded his eyes but the line of his mouth definitely fit her description. Uptight and unfriendly. "You were introduced as Diana Young. *Do* I know you?"

"After my husband died it was easier to keep his name. Plus there are advantages to not carrying the Fielding name around…not that it matters. I'm still me."

"Well, there's the thing," he said in his deep, down-under drawl. "I don't know that I ever knew you."

That shocked a short, astonished laugh from Diana. Never in her thirty-one years had she been as honest, as open, as *herself,* as in the time she'd spent as Max's lover. "How can you say that? I shared everything with you!"

"Yeah, you shared. That's what I don't appreciate, Mrs. Young. That's why I'm not feeling as friendly toward you as I used to."

"What do you mean?" Diana shook her head slowly. "What on earth do you think I shared?"

"Your body, mostly. How did Mr. Young like that?"

"Are you implying that I was already married?" she asked with rising incredulity.

"Not married, but you must have been engaged."

"I wasn't."

"You expect me to believe you met and married this Young character less than three weeks after leaving me? I guess it must have been love at first sight, then."

Diana reared back, stung by the bitter irony of his accusation. Love at first sight had been Max. Her marriage to David Young, a big, inescapable, back-firing disaster. She'd always guarded the details closely because she knew what the gossip media would make of it. And because she didn't enjoy admitting to the naivety and weakness that had opened her up to emotional blackmail, to the power she'd allowed her father and David Young to exert over her.

At one time she would have shared those details with Max—she'd called him, Lord knows, she'd tried. But not now. Not after those coldly delivered accusations.

Instead she fastened on the other untruth in his argument. "I didn't leave you, Max. I went home because I had to…and only after we agreed that we saw our relationship somewhat differently. You wanted sex, I wanted more."

He stared at her a moment, no sign of giving in the hard set of his face. It was the same uncompromising expression as the night they'd quarreled, when she'd realized how woefully she'd misconstrued their relationship. "You wanted to get married that bad?" he asked now. "That you said yes to the first batter up after I walked away from the plate?"

"It wasn't like that," she fired back. "David was my father's business partner. I didn't agree to marry him for the sake of a wedding band, okay?"

His lips compressed into a straight line of condemnation, and Diana realized that her angry outburst added weight to his belief she'd been involved with David all along. She thought about rephrasing but what did it matter? Driving here today she'd cautioned herself about getting involved again. She did not need this old heartache.

"My relationship with you was over when I returned to New York and you didn't bother to acknowledge my calls," she said, mustering some dignity and wrapping it around her like a protective cloak. "It's been ten years. Why are we rehashing old quarrels?"

"You brought it up."

"And, frankly, I'm sorry I did."

"Seems we agree on one thing."

For a long moment Diana couldn't find any comeback, and to her horror she felt the ache of tears building at the back of her throat. She couldn't do this. She couldn't pretend emotional detachment any more than she'd been able to ten years before.

"It seems that I've come to agree with you on another point." She swallowed against the painful lump that was making it so dashed difficult to maintain her dignity. "I don't believe I'm the right photographer for this job after all."

"Suit yourself." He gave a curt shrug. "You're not indispensable, Diana. I can find a replacement."

Glutton for punishment, she had to ask. "Is that what

you did after I left Australia? Is that why you never returned my calls?"

He paused in opening the stable door, close enough now that she could see the wintry chill of his eyes and beneath the green patina a hint of some deeper emotion. Pain? Regret? Frustration? He shut the door behind him with a thud of finality and whatever she'd thought she'd seen was gone.

"Something like that," he said in answer to her question. Then he touched his hat in a cowboy's salute of farewell and walked away.

Two

"Is there something wrong with your lunch?"

Diana blinked until the chicken breast she'd been worrying around her plate came into focus. "No, it's fine."

"And you know this," Eliza asked, "because…?"

Trust her friend to point out the obvious. Diana gave up on her untouched meal and put down her silverware. "I shouldn't have let you talk me into this."

This happened to be a late lunch in the atrium restaurant at the Fortune's Seven Hotel. The hotel's ballroom was the scene of next month's Historical Society Auction to raise funds for reparations to the city's Old West Museum. The fundraising committee, chaired by Eliza, had met earlier to discuss the function with hotel staff, and Eliza had used her gently persuasive charm to cajole Diana into lunch and a shopping expedition afterward.

"I'm not good company today," Diana added.

"You don't say."

Diana pulled a face at her friend's dry comment and watched her eyes turn serious as she, too, abandoned her entrée and leaned back in her chair. Eliza waited for the wait-staff to remove their plates before skewering her with the million-dollar question.

"I don't suppose this would have anything to do with my Aussie cousin?"

"Would you believe me if I said no?"

"No. At Case's party I could have cut the tension between you two with a butter knife, and I get the feeling you've been sidestepping me ever since. You know I'm dying to hear details. Come on," Eliza coaxed, leaning forward in her chair again. "Spill."

As usual, Eliza was right. Diana had been avoiding her friend's curiosity and now she wished she hadn't been such a coward. After this morning's altercation with Max, today had to be the worst possible time for the explanation she owed her best friend. But she did owe Eliza the details she begged, so she might as well get it over and done.

"We met at a party in Australia," she began, jumping into the deep end. "On the trip I took after we graduated from Wellesley."

Eliza digested this for a moment, shock evident in her blue eyes. "I gave you the contact number for my Aussie relations. You met them and you didn't say a word?"

"I'm sorry, Eliza, truly I am. I didn't meet any of your family except Max, and I didn't mean to keep him a secret. I just didn't know *how* to tell you I was having a hot and heavy affair with your cousin. I knew you'd want details and I couldn't talk about something I didn't understand. I don't even know that I can explain what happened between us now! Then I came home and married David…"

"And your life fell to pieces," Eliza finished softly after Diana's attempted explanation trailed off.

Their gazes met for a second, remembering the anguish of those years after her forced marriage, when Diana had cut herself off from all her friends. Yet Eliza, her roommate at Wellesley, had continued to send Christmas gifts and birthday cards, and when she'd read about David's death in a newspaper, she'd flown out to California for the funeral.

After the service she'd learned the whole sorry story of Diana's marriage. She met David's sons, too, and when their attempts to prevent Diana taking anything from her marriage grew vindictive, she'd invited Diana to visit her in Sioux Falls. Diana had only returned to California to pack her things. Her move to Sioux Falls and all the good, confidence-building, independence-gaining things that ensued were all due to Eliza's friendship.

"I'm sorry." Diana's second apology vibrated with regret and the threat of tears. "I should have told you about Max."

"That the hound dog hit on you at a party? Perhaps it's better you didn't!"

Diana managed to smile at Eliza's teasing remark despite the ache in her chest. That was the thing about her friend—she had a gift of measuring the mood and choosing the perfect moment to lighten the tone. "I think it's fair to say that the hitting-on was a mutual thing. Remember when we studied French? Remember how we mocked the drama of the *coup de foudre?*"

"The stroke of lightning," Eliza murmured. "Love at first sight."

"I know it's a romantic cliché, but when I met Max I actually experienced that lightning strike. The ground shifted. Time stood still then raced through six and a half weeks. I didn't know how to explain that to anyone, Eliza, and I had this self-centered desire to hug it to myself."

"Do I gather it ended badly?" Eliza asked.

"However did you guess?"

"The day Max arrived, he was so laidback and charming. I knew you had to meet him, which is why I called and made sure you were coming to the party. I had a notion you two would get along. But then I introduced you and he couldn't raise a smile. It was so unlike him." Eliza's reached across the table and put her hand over Diana's, perhaps because she'd noticed the wobble in her composure. "You know I was only teasing about spilling details. You don't have to tell me anything that's too upsetting."

"I have no reason to be upset," Diana replied quickly. "Except seeing him again has me all churned up with the bad part of the memories more than the good." But after taking a deep breath, she wanted to share, to ease the angst that had been building ever since he'd walked away from her that morning in the barn. "I had extended my holiday once and Father was making noises about needing me at home. I didn't know what was going on and selfishly I didn't want to know. I didn't want to leave Australia—I didn't want to leave Max—and so I pushed him for a reason to stay."

"He didn't want you to stay?"

"Let's just say he didn't appreciate me pressuring him for commitment or acting shrewish over the number of ex-girlfriends who called. I should have read the signs right there, but I didn't."

Eliza winced in sympathy. "No one wants to be one of many."

"I suppose not and with Max there was quite the backlist. Apparently he'd been sized up as marriage material once too often and I made the same mistake. So we quarreled and he left on a business trip and while he was away everything hit the fan with my sister. I had to catch a flight home that day and I didn't even know where Max had gone. I left a note and a message on his service and I called again from New York."

Her shrug said the rest and Eliza's clasp on her hand tightened. "He didn't return your calls?"

"I ended up contacting his neighbor, who I'd met in passing. He told me Max had gone to this big outback race-meeting that lasted all week—not work, but a party! Oh, and he knew because Max had taken his sister, Eva." Diana smiled gamely but the bitter ache of that discovery, of that whole horrendous week, squeezed like a fisted hand around her heart. "Can you believe I expected we had more from a holiday fling? Can you believe I was that naive?"

"Coup de foudre."

"Oh, I thought so at the time, but who believes in love at first sight?"

"It happens," Eliza surprised her by saying. Her expression had turned somber, and Diana had the feeling she was thinking of something else. Or someone else. But a moment later she shed that introspective look and smiled brightly. "You know, I think this discussion needs uplifting with something decadent."

"Crème brûlée?"

"Cheesecake."

Diana wasn't convinced she could force even dessert past the tightness in her throat and chest, but she pretended to study the menu while that morning's conversation with Max replayed through her mind. "You know what *is* upsetting me?" she asked after several minutes of stewing. "This morning he accused me of playing around with him while I was engaged to David."

Eliza put down her menu. "Why on earth would he think that?"

"Because I married so quickly."

"Did you tell him why?"

Diana shook her head. "I couldn't see any point. He was so rude and presumptive. He assumed the wedding was all set before I went to Australia."

After a moment's contemplation, Eliza asked, "How did he know when you actually married David? If he never contacted you after you returned home…."

"I suppose he must have read about the wedding—it was in a lot of magazines. David made sure of that. Not that it matters how Max knew. I just don't understand why he's so antagonistic. Especially after so much time."

"Perhaps he's suffering from dog-in-manger syndrome. He didn't want to marry you himself, but that didn't mean he wanted someone else to."

"That's crazy!"

"That's men." Eliza gave a rueful shrug. "I grew up with three brothers. Believe me, the competitiveness extends into all kinds of craziness."

The waiter returned to take their orders and Diana laid her menu on the table. "I'm going to pass," she said. "I have some prints to make this afternoon."

"You're not coming shopping? I was relying on you to help me choose an outfit for Case and Gina's wedding." Eliza gave the menu one last look of longing then handed it to their waiter. "I'm afraid I'll have to pass, as well, or I'll never find anything to fit." She turned back to Diana. "You haven't forgotten the wedding is this weekend?"

"No."

"No…but?" Eliza asked, astutely reading the hint of more in her answer.

"Will your visitors from 'down under' be there?"

"I believe so. Zack is heading home to New Zealand the next day but Max is staying on for another week or so. Surely you're not letting this spat with him change your plans?"

"Not seeing him again would prevent any more spats."

"Didn't you decide when you moved here," her friend pointed out with quiet gravity, "that this new start was about taking control of your life? That you wouldn't allow yourself to be manipulated or managed any more?"

"This isn't the same thing."

"As the games your father and husband played? No. But is staying home and hiding from your past the best way to move forward? I think you should go to the wedding. And I think you should come shopping." A devilish smile sparked Eliza's eyes. "We'll find a knockout dress that makes you feel fabulous and—bonus points—makes my dog-in-manger cousin sit up and howl at the moon!"

Diana laughed at the image, even as she shook her head. "I don't need a new outfit."

On a roll, Eliza didn't listen. "It would be even better if you took a date."

"There's no one I—"

Eliza snapped her fingers. "Jeffrey!"

"My boss, Jeffrey? Oh, no. We don't date."

"Not strictly, but you do have those dinner nondates."

"As friends and colleagues," Diana pointed out.

"So invite him as your friend and colleague. You know how Jeffrey adores any opportunity to promote his gallery. This is the perfect opportunity. And since he's good-looking, single and a terrific dancer, he is also the perfect date." Satisfied with her logic, Eliza picked up her purse and signaled the waiter. "Now that's decided, let's go find us both the perfect dress!"

It wasn't the dress that made Max sit up and take notice, although it had taken him a decent slice of the wedding reception to work that out. At first he thought it was the color, a rich sapphire blue that provided the ideal foil for her dark hair and creamy skin. Then he saw her walking and decided it was the way the layers of fabric faithfully flowed with the sway of her hips. And when she danced the subtle sprinkling of sequins only glinted beneath the ballroom chandeliers when others around her dazzled.

This wasn't a dress that screamed look-at-me. Oh no, it whispered in a sultry midnight voice to check out the body inside. *That's* what had made him sit up and take notice.

"Some dress, isn't it?"

Max blinked his focus away from the dancers to frown at his companion. What the hell was Zack doing checking out Diana's dress? Except it wasn't Diana who'd nailed his mate's attention, he realized belatedly, but a woman standing nearby. Until she turned her laughing face their way he didn't recognize the feminine figure in green as his cousin Skylar, but that's who it was all right. The down-to-earth tomboy he'd teasingly nicknamed Freckles was all glammed up and, yes, even wearing a dress.

No wonder Zack had noticed…although he wasn't sure he liked the way his mate was eyeing her. "I think it's time to hit the dance-floor," Zack murmured.

"Good idea. Here, hold this." Max pressed his empty champagne flute into Zack's hand. Ignoring the indignant protest, he winked and clapped his friend on the back. "It's every man for himself. See you out there."

"You're not such a bad dancer, cuzz," Sky teased. "For an Aussie cowhand."

"It became a lot easier when you gave up fighting me for the lead, Freckles."

She laughed and punched his arm lightly before resuming their comfortable two-step. "What do you think of our wedding, South Dakota style?"

"I'm amazed they put this shindig together so quickly." Only three weeks ago Case had stunned everyone by announcing his engagement to Gina Reynolds, yet they'd managed to pull off a smoothly run and stylish event with a seeming lack of effort.

"When Case sets his mind to something, there's no stopping him," Sky remarked. "Plus it helps that he owns the venue."

Max grinned at that wry observation. "No doubt."

The venue was the spectacular ballroom of the Fortune's Seven Hotel, part of the diverse portfolio of businesses put together by Nash Fortune and his father before him and his father before him. Since Nash's early retirement, Dakota Fortune had been run from an impressive downtown office complex by Case and his brother Creed, who'd continued to build the company's considerable assets.

Creed, Max noted, had stood up as best man for his elder brother while Blake, the third of Nash's sons, had been a conspicuous absentee from the wedding ceremony.

In the weeks since their arrival Max and Zack had spent a lot of time jetting to and fro—sometimes with Skylar along to provide local expertise—inspecting stud complexes from Nebraska to Kentucky to Florida. In between trips Max had met all his cousins. He'd dined with them, shared early breakfasts and late suppers with those who lived at the big estate house, but until this evening he hadn't picked up on all the underlying family tensions.

Point in question, the current heated discussion between Creed and Blake, who had just arrived at the hotel. Creed's date was attempting to conciliate. Max hoped her evening dress was flame retardant.

"You've gone quiet," Sky said. "Are you enjoying yourself?"

"Let's say I'm being entertained."

Noticing what had prompted his dry remark, she clicked her tongue in admonishment. "For Gina's sake, I hope they don't come to blows."

"Do they often?"

"Not since Blake moved out of the house. He has some issues with the way Case and Creed cut him out of the family business."

"I hear he's done very well on his own."

"Extremely well. His casinos are worth a bomb, which is all the more reason he should let this stuff go." The frown puckering Sky's brow deepened to a scowl. "Perhaps I should go and crack their stubborn male heads together."

"You'll only draw more attention. Besides, Creed's girlfriend looks like she has them in hand."

"Would you look at that? They're walking off in separate directions, and I don't think Case and Gina even noticed!" She breathed a sigh of relief and relaxed again. "I heard Sasha was very good at her job. Have you met her? She's a public relations assistant at Dakota Fortune."

"I haven't, but after that display I'd like to."

"I heard you had a rep as a lady's man. 'The Playboy Cowboy', isn't it?"

Heard from Zack, no doubt. His friend thought the

society columnist's ridiculous tag was a real hoot. Max shook his head in mock disillusionment. "I can't believe you'd take the word of that silver-tongued Kiwi over your own flesh-and-blood relation."

Oddly, she didn't fire back her usual smart mouth response. Max noticed the slight flush creeping into her face. *Uh-oh.* "I should warn you about Zack…."

"I should warn you about Sasha," Sky retorted. "She's with Creed."

"My interest is only in her PR skills."

"Sure it is."

Max chuckled and didn't bother defending himself further. He did like women but his teasing banter with Sky was only that. A bit of fun that helped divert his attention from the only woman who had captured his interest tonight.

That woman wasn't Creed's auburn-haired date, despite her impressive peacemaking performance.

A tap on his shoulder brought their dance to a halt and he turned to find Maya Blackstone apologizing for the interruption. Maya was the daughter of Nash Fortune's third and current wife, Patricia, with striking looks that affirmed her Native American heritage. From what he'd gathered while living at the Fortune estate, Maya was a close friend of Skylar's but maintained a cool distance from the rest of her step-siblings.

Maya turned a worried face to Sky. "Have you seen my mother? I've looked everywhere and can't find her. She was so quiet earlier—I'm worried she may be ill."

"She wasn't feeling well," Sky confirmed. "A

headache, I think. She said she was going home before it got any worse, but she didn't want anyone to fuss."

"But that's so unlike her," Maya fussed regardless. "You know she hates missing any part of a family celebration."

"Well, at least she missed Creed and Blake's latest altercation. That wouldn't have helped her headache any!"

"Oh, please, tell me you're joking."

"Problem?"

They all turned at Zack's intrusion, and Max lost interest in Maya and Sky's exchange about the warring half-brothers when he saw Diana at his friend's side. Her hand remained in Zack's, as if they'd paused in dancing to join the little huddle at the edge of the dance-floor.

That niggled at him a cursed sight more than all the dances she'd shared with her date.

Max had observed her interaction with that smooth customer all evening without detecting any spark of heat. The bloke was attentive as a lapdog and they seemed comfortable together. Obviously they were friends but he'd bet London to a brick they weren't lovers.

His New Zealand buddy, however, had to be watched. Zack pulled women with a scary lack of effort—that's what he'd wanted to warn Sky about. Perhaps he should have warned Zack to keep his hands off both his cousin *and* Diana!

A third man joined their group and Maya introduced him as her boyfriend Brad McKenzie, before filling him in on Patricia's whereabouts. Apparently he'd been helping Maya in her search and now he took her hand and towed her onto the dance-floor. During the round of introductions and explanations, Zack had struck up a conversation with Sky and they, too, took to the floor.

Zack didn't miss the chance to wink and mouth *every man for himself* as he departed.

Max reminded himself that Sky was capable of holding her own in any company. She also had a father and three big brothers to watch out for her. Besides, he'd been left alone with Diana and that realization brought an edgy satisfaction that overrode everything else.

All evening she'd managed to evade his company. Not that he blamed her. He'd had just enough champagne to admit that he could have handled their last encounter with more finesse. He hoped he'd had enough champagne to manage an apology.

"Are you enjoying yourself?" she asked with cool politeness, still avoiding eye contact.

"It's been…interesting."

"In what way?"

"Keeping up with all the crosscurrents has been an exercise," he admitted. "I can understand Patricia's headache."

A small smile tugged at the corner of her mouth. "Fortune parties are never dull."

"This one hasn't been," he said softly. "And that smile of yours just made it even brighter."

He heard the little hitch in her breath, saw the flutter of pulse in her throat, and finally her gaze swung up to connect with his. In that instant there was no pretense, no anger, just the intense familiarity of this woman, of that look in her eyes, of how she'd fit in his arms, in his bed, in his life.

All the years they'd spent apart fell away like a tumbling house of cards. Whether it was the moment, the setting, the champagne, it didn't matter. He knew that he still wanted her and chance had delivered the perfect opportunity to have her in his arms again.

When he took her hand, the kick of contact resonated through his body and hummed in his blood. He felt the slight tremble in her fingertips a split second before she tried to pull away, but he fastened his grip and tugged her nearer.

Her eyes widened in surprise and she puffed out a gasp of indignation. "What do you think you are doing?"

"Resuming the dance Maya interrupted," he said, pulling her resistive body into the traditional waltz hold. "Since your partner abandoned you, looks like you're stuck with me."

Three

Finding herself so unexpectedly alone with Max—with a Max who traded quips and flattering charm rather than backhanded swipes about her marriage—had thrown Diana for a loop before he took her hand and set her fingertips alive with sensation. It took two seconds of that skin-to-skin contact to admit that she'd never responded so instantly and intensely to any other man.

Not before Max, not since Max.

She was still off balance and struggling for composure when he attempted to lead her into the waltz steps that matched an old orchestral standard. His hand on her back seared through the filmy fabric to imprint the skin beneath. Hormones that had perked to life with the first glimpse of his smile now soared to their own melody.

Yet her feet dragged, heavy with I-can't-do-this-all-over-again fear and reluctance.

Around them other couples took evasive action, and her obvious resistance was drawing curious glances. To stand her ground and demand he let her go would only bring more attention to herself, something she'd loathed since childhood. With a stage diva mother and Broadway director father, she and her sisters had been expected to not only share their parents' limelight but to revel in it.

Somehow Diana had missed out on those particular genes.

One of the reasons she'd fallen in love with photography was because it placed her on the other side of the spotlight; one of the talents she brought to her craft was her understanding of stage fright. She worked hard to devise settings that put her subjects at ease, and she helped them by using the same disassociation and relaxation techniques that had pulled her through an unhappy adolescence and even unhappier marriage.

Now seemed a perfect time to apply those skills.

Closing her eyes, she concentrated on the music, letting the rhythm flow through her limbs and into the dance steps. After several minutes and a complete circle of the spacious ballroom floor, she had almost blocked out her partner. And then he spoke.

"Not so hard, is it, once you relax and go with the flow."

"I started lessons when I was three." Following a strong male lead had never been an issue for her. Allowing herself to be pushed and pulled had been her strong—or weak—suit. "Dancing isn't the problem."

Max had always been sharp; she didn't need to state out loud that *he* was the problem. His mouth kicked into a rueful half-smile. "I guess I deserved that."

"For railroading me into dancing with you? Yes."

"If I'd gone the formal route and asked you for the pleasure of this dance, would you have accepted?"

"No."

"It's only a dance," he pointed out.

"Is it?"

He regarded her silently for a moment. "What do you think it is, Diana?"

Not *Mrs. Young.* In fact he was being altogether too affable. She didn't trust him or the lingering traces of his smile any more than she trusted her body's extravagant responses to his nearness. She didn't need her breasts pointing out their acute craving; she didn't want these touch-me flutters suffusing her skin. "I have no idea what this is," she said archly. "Given your antagonism the last two occasions we've met, I can't help but wonder what this civility is all about."

"You think I have an agenda?"

"I think you have a nerve, expecting me to take pleasure in your company."

"Would an apology help?"

"For the other morning? Oh, I think it would take a lot more than 'sorry' to make up for that outlandish allegation!"

Diana had set out for the late afternoon wedding determined on three fronts. To enjoy herself, no matter how many bad memories the ceremony evoked. To ignore Max, no matter how fine he looked in a formal suit. And if the second failed, to not get involved in another altercation.

So much for good intentions.

She'd been so focused on blocking out the impact of his touch, his scent, his sexy drawl—and that damn lopsided smile!—that she'd allowed herself to be sucked into this dialogue with less resistance than she'd given his request for a dance.

Now she waltzed on with her heart in her throat, dreading an offhand and meaningless apology as much as she feared further harsh words. But he didn't reply for a long while, during which he turned her expertly to avoid another couple—Zack and Skylar, she noticed, absorbed in their own conversation—and in the process he managed to shift his grip and ease her closer into the protective shield of his body.

For a moment she forgot herself and her resistance in the smooth slide of his jacket beneath her fingers and the memory of his smooth, hot skin beneath. Then he spoke, so close to her ear that the deep timbre of his voice took on a life of its own in her blood. Battling her way back from those sensory depths, it took a little while for the ambiguity of his response to register.

I'll keep that in mind.

That's what he'd said. But what did he mean? That an apology wouldn't be worth the effort…or that he'd need to put in more effort?

Diana wasn't sure she wanted to know the answer, yet not knowing left her feeling off-kilter and dissatisfied, like when a movie ended too suddenly without tying up all the threads. For a while she fostered that resentment of a story left unfinished. Would it have hurt him to explain himself and his changed attitude? Would it have been too much for him to attempt an apology?

Honestly? Yes. She knew him well enough to answer her own questions. Max Fortune had never been one for fake sentiments or for long-winded explanations. He made decisions, he acted, and those actions did the speaking for him.

Perhaps he didn't have an agenda.

Perhaps, because of their errant partners, he'd simply found himself in a situation where he felt he should ask her to dance. Except asking would have resulted in a rebuff so he'd acted....

"It's only a dance," she murmured, repeating his earlier words to close the conversation in her own mind.

But he'd heard, apparently, because he leaned back a little, enough that he could look down into her face. "I've changed my mind about that," he said. "It's not only a dance. It's our first dance."

"Is it?" she asked, as if she hadn't known, as if that hadn't registered the instant he'd swung her into his arms.

"Yeah." The same crooked smile as earlier touched his lips, but there was a dark gravity in his expression that caused her heartbeat to slow and deepen. "Seems we never got around to actual dates. Maybe that's something else I need to apologize for."

"That's not necessary," she told him.

Dating hadn't been necessary, either, she thought with a bittersweet jab of memory. She'd fallen straight into his bed the night they'd met. Sure, they'd gone out for plenty of meals but those had always ended in a giddy rush home when they couldn't keep their hands off each other any longer.

It was only after her return to New York, when she'd waited anxiously for a call that never came, that she'd taken an unblinkered look at her status in his life. No visits to meet his family. No double dates with his friends. Dancing with Zack earlier, she'd been stunned to learn that he and Max had been friends since university. As entrepreneurial partners they'd started up a range of ventures from the time they graduated, and yet she'd never met Zack and he knew nothing of her.

What a way to be reminded of her place in Max's life!

It helped, reminding herself that their relationship had started and ended between the sheets. It even helped that she knew the same attraction still existed. She'd matured enough to recognize the chemistry for what it was and to handle it with her poise intact.

The past ten minutes had proven that, if nothing else. She could dance with him, trade quips with him, stand her ground with him, and walk away at the end of a dance.

It *is* just a dance, she told herself with a new and confident resolve.

And although the physical responses she felt with every brush of his thigh and every tightening of his hand around hers were real and strong and underpinned by memories of her first love affair—her only love affair—they were only physical responses. That was all she would allow them to be. She would walk away with her shoulders straight and her head held high.

In less than a week Max Fortune would be gone and

her life would continue, as it had done all those years ago, except this time there would be no regrets.

The dance ended a few minutes later with the announcement that Mr. and Mrs. Case Fortune were leaving the reception to start their new life together as man and wife. The promise in those words hit Diana hard. It was, she realized with chagrin, compounded by the fact that Max had not let her go when the music ended.

While the M.C. took the mic and called for the guests' attention, his hand was doing this stroking thing across the small of her back. For some silly reason that heedless caress intensified her ache of aloneness and she had to fight the urge to turn into his solid strength.

But she didn't. She wouldn't.

Extricating herself from his hold, she managed a smile and a polite thank you for the dance before they were joined at the edge of the gathering guests by Eliza and Jeffrey.

"There you are. I thought I'd lost you." Her boss/friend/date claimed her side with a possessiveness that caught Diana by surprise. What was he up to? Eyebrows raised, his gaze slid from her to Max and back in a way that begged an introduction.

Eliza obliged and they swapped small talk about the evening's success and then about Max's travels in the weeks he'd been in America. Despite Jeffrey's proprietary grip on her arm, Diana started to relax. Perhaps she'd looked in need of rescuing. Perhaps Eliza had set him up to act the role of neglected date.

Looking on the bright side, she could now say good

night and escape Max's company. That had to be a good thing.

"Not entering into the spirit of the bouquet toss?" Jeffrey asked, startling her out of silent contemplation. Then she realized his question was for Eliza who, unusually, seemed lost for an answer.

"A public tussle for a bunch of flowers? I can't imagine that being Eliza's thing. Much too undignified." Max slung a friendly arm around his cousin's shoulder. "Am I right, Blondie?"

Eliza narrowed her eyes at him. "Did you just call me *Blondie?* Because that's something I might get into a public tussle over!"

Laughter and more teasing followed, but Diana noticed that Max squeezed his cousin's shoulder before he let her go. It seemed a small thing, that gesture of support, but it took a special empathy to detect the need for comfort and that reminded Diana of the man she'd fallen for all those years ago. Not the man with the smooth seduction skills, not the ardent, patient, skillful lover, but the man who knew how to sooth a nervous woman as easily as he soothed a fractious horse.

A loud cheer went up, signaling that one of the singletons had won the tussle for Gina's bouquet and allowing Diana the moment she needed to swallow the bittersweet taste of regret.

"The party here will be winding down now the formalities are over," Eliza said brightly. "Why don't you come back to the estate? I'm sure we can scare up a liqueur or a coffee or even another bottle of champagne."

"What do you say, Diana?" Jeffrey asked. "Shall we kick on for a bit or would you prefer to go straight home?"

It shouldn't have been a difficult question. Jeffrey had presented two clearly-stated choices. Problem was, she felt the weight of Max's silent scrutiny and her simple decision grew infinitely more complex. From Eliza she'd learned that he was staying at the big house, in a spare apartment on the third floor. Which meant he would, most likely, be at the small after-party gathering.

"Well?" Eliza prompted, "what *do* you say, Diana?"

There was something in her friend's tone of voice that reminded Diana that she'd vowed to make decisions based on her own desires. She'd proven during the dance that she didn't have to avoid him. She could handle the heat of attraction and she could handle the emotional backdraft, and it felt good to acknowledge that strength in herself. Her self-confidence had taken too many knocks for her not to celebrate its moments of power.

"I say it's much too early to call it a night." With a smile, she linked her arm through Jeffrey's. "We'd love to come out to the estate," she told Eliza. "Especially if you can scare up that champagne you mentioned."

It was well past midnight and the informal party had thinned to a sprinkling of family and close friends, most of them gathered around the stone fireplace in the Fortune's great room. Max would have called it a night himself if not for one small detail.

Diana.

All he needed was a piece of her time, alone, to deliver an apology and whatever else was needed to convince her it wasn't over between them. He could have done the first during their dance, while the indignation flared in her eyes and stiffened her pretty spine. But she'd demanded more than *I'm sorry* and it had taken a while to figure out what he could offer.

Now he was impatient to put his strategy into action.

Half an hour earlier Diana had left the great room with Eliza and Sasha, apparently to inspect one of Eliza's interior design projects. Nash had returned early to check on his wife's health as a headache had caused her to leave the reception before him. Maya's departure a short while ago—after an intense head-to-head with Creed over his half brother, Blake—left an all-male group and the conversation, naturally, had turned to sport. Not that he didn't appreciate the hell out of sports, but the discussion had shifted from football to hockey and he was well and truly in the dark.

"Hockey not your game?"

Max turned to find Creed at his elbow. "It's not big in Australia," he told his cousin. "We don't have the ice."

"The game goes better on ice," Creed deadpanned. Then, "I was talking to your friend Zack at the wedding. He said you both played football, back in your college days."

"That's how we met," Max confirmed. "On opposing sides of a ruck."

Creed raised his eyebrows at the unfamiliar word.

"A rugby term," Max explained. "That's the football we played, first on opposing teams and later we played together…which proved much better for our friendship."

"I expected to see Zack out here tonight."

"So did I, but he flies home tomorrow. I guess he decided he needed an early night."

Max swallowed the last of his port and put down his glass.

"Are you heading upstairs?" Creed asked.

"Soon." Max's gaze drifted to the door, to where the women had disappeared earlier. "After I say my goodnights."

His cousin's eyes narrowed astutely as he read between the lines. "Ah." He nodded solemnly. "Good luck."

Had his interest in Diana been so obvious? By the knowing—and possibly sympathetic—twinkle in Creed's eyes, the answer was yes. And Max didn't much care. He grinned and clapped his cousin on the back. "Thanks, mate. I think I'm going to need that luck and then some."

The lilting warmth of female laughter led him straight to the library room, where the three women looked up guiltily at his arrival. Eliza gave an audible sigh of relief. "Thank heavens it's not Creed." She waved a hand at the album open on her lap. "He'd have a cow if he knew I was showing Sasha his nude-on-a-rug baby pictures."

"I thought I'd find you oohing and aahing over cushions and curtains and color schemes," he said, "not baby pictures."

"And yet you still came through the door?" Eliza's brows arched in faux shock. "My, but you're brave."

"Is the party breaking up?" Sasha asked.

"Winding down. Unless you have an opinion on this year's Stanley Cup. That'd kick things on a bit longer."

"You walked out on a sports discussion?" Eliza shook her head. "Are you ill?"

"I wanted to catch Diana before she left."

His gaze shifted to where she sat on the deep red sofa, shoes kicked off, long legs tucked up beneath her. If his request alarmed her, it didn't show. She looked comfortable, poised, and so damn beautiful he felt the kick in his solar plexus.

"Well, Sasha, do you want to brave the hockey debate?" Eliza closed the thick book and set it aside. "If that's all right with you, Diana?"

"Of course it is," she affirmed after the briefest hint of hesitation. "But please let Jeffrey know I'll be ready for home in a few minutes."

Max waited by the door while the women slipped on shoes and said their farewells. On her way out Eliza paused, and in the guise of bussing his cheek murmured, "Behave yourself, cousin."

He had little choice, given Diana's reminder that her date-on-a-leash was waiting the command to take her home. That message might have been directed to Eliza, but Max knew the point was aimed right at him. He knew and it sat all kinds of uncomfortable as he closed the door behind Eliza.

"A few minutes," he mused, turning to Diana who sat straight-backed, shoes now on her feet, hands folded primly in her lap. No longer relaxed but still kick-gut beautiful. "Is that all the time you have for me, Diana?"

She lifted her chin, as cool and regal as any princess. "What do you want, Max?"

Right at that minute, he wanted to muss up her ice-princess demeanor. Preferably with his hands and his mouth. He debated telling her so, but decided that it wouldn't help his cause. He wanted to smooth things over, to win back some measure of her trust, not resume their verbal fisticuffs. "I want to talk."

"About?"

"The other morning, at the stables." Their eyes locked and held. He hated explanations and justifications, but this had to be done. "You caught me off guard, turning up as you did. I didn't even know you lived in Sioux Falls."

"You'd seen me at the party weeks before."

"I thought you were visiting Eliza."

A frown of annoyance drew her serious dark brows together. "If you'd bothered to stay long enough to speak to me, you'd have found out otherwise."

"So tell me now," he said evenly, ignoring the bite in her voice. "How long have you lived in Sioux Falls?"

"I moved here three years ago."

"May I ask why?"

She lifted a shoulder, then let it drop. "After my husband died, I wanted a change."

"I guess you got that."

Her eyes narrowed, suspicious of his meaning. "I've gotten exactly what I was looking for when I decided to leave Beverly Hills. Sioux Falls is quiet and relaxed and friendly, yet it has every service and facility a person could ask for."

"It's a long way from Manhattan and Beverly Hills."

"Yes, but I never enjoyed living in either of those places. And if I do need to visit, we do have an airport here."

"You can go anywhere from here," he said, quoting a slogan he'd heard more than once during his travels.

"I prefer to take that as a positive."

"Hey, I agree." Max held up his hands in mock protection against her sharp tone. Like a tigress defending her adopted home. He liked that a whole lot more than the ice-princess act. "That's how Nash convinced us to stay here. By private jet we can fly pretty much anywhere for the day."

Mollified, she settled back in her corner of the sofa but her eyes remained wary as they watched him move closer. "Did that work out?" she asked after he'd settled his hips against the mahogany table in the center of the room.

"Better than expected. We've had no delays or shutdowns."

"Then you have been lucky. That's part of winter in South Dakota."

"Part of the appeal?" he asked, tongue-in-cheek.

A small smile curved her lips but he sensed a seriousness in her eyes as she said, "Yes, as it happens."

"Too much California sun?"

"Too much California."

The comment, delivered as a breezy counter to his quip, seemed to develop weight and significance in the beat of silence that followed. Her mouth tightened with vexation, as if she regretted giving away something telling. Something Max had to follow up... "You weren't happy living there?"

She puffed out a small breath. "Does that please you?"

"Should it?"

"Given the tone of your commentary on my marriage last week at the stables, I'd say yes."

"I don't want to talk about your marriage," he said shortly. Hell, he couldn't think about it without feeling the bitter jab of betrayal. Knowledge of her unhappiness did nothing to ease that.

"You said you wanted to talk about the other morning, at the stables."

"Correct." Max pushed his hands into his trouser pockets and fixed her with an unflinching look. "You were engaged by Sky to do a job. You should have had the chance to complete it."

Mention of the photography job had thrown her. He could see that in her eyes, in the frown between them. "From memory," she said slowly, "I chose to not take the job."

"You said you weren't the right person."

"Because that's the impression you gave when you questioned my suitability. Good grief, Max, you even had the nerve to pass judgment on my choice of clothing!"

"So, you do want the job?"

Caught out by his question, she blinked slowly. "I thought you would have found someone else by now."

"No."

She moistened her lips and Max smiled with satisfaction deep inside. She wanted the job, all right. He saw it in that unconscious gesture and in the equally hungry glow in her eyes. Pride—and wariness of his motives—might not allow her to admit it, however.

"When do you want the work done?" she asked.

"I need the prints by Friday."

She nodded. "Eliza said you were going home next weekend."

"I was, but that's not the case now. I'm staying on a while longer. There's some unfinished business I need to attend to."

Suspicion flickered in the shadowed depths of her eyes. "Business with the horses?"

Max took a second to contemplate his answer, a second when the tension of their own unfinished business, of all they'd left unsaid or should have left unsaid, crackled between them in the midnight-quiet room.

"We made an offer on a stallion," he told her, sticking to the business facts. "The owners have yet to see reason on a price. They will."

She laughed at that, a wry response that sounded part relief and part rebuke. "Do you still always get everything you go after?"

Jagged memories of another wedding day, of a diamond ring in his pocket and an empty seat beside him on the long flight home, sliced through Max's senses.

No, he hadn't always succeeded in what he'd gone after.

"Not always," he said with a tight shrug. "Sometimes it takes longer than anticipated…and sometimes I change my mind about what I want."

He wasn't talking about horses now. He was talking about the unfinished business of their attraction, and thinking how this time there would be no talk of weddings and commitment, no second travel booking, no diamond ring in his pocket.

This time would only be a holiday fling, the same as the first time should have been.

Once he got her back in his bed….

Conviction burned deep and steady and low in his gut as he met her eyes. "The photography job is yours, Diana, if you want it."

"Is this your way of apologizing?" she asked, still wary, still suspicious.

"It's my way of admitting I was wrong to let you walk away from a promised job." Straightening from the desk, he held out his hand. "Do we have a deal?"

Four

Of course Diana wanted the job. And of course she took it, despite the niggling concern that Max's unfinished business in Sioux Falls involved more than horse-dealing. Every time she recalled the dark gleam of satisfaction in his eyes when she'd said yes, her apprehension grew.

What, exactly, had she shaken hands on?

Several times on Sunday she picked up the phone, intent on demanding an explanation. But then she asked herself if his motivation mattered. She wanted the job; she should take it. She didn't want anything beyond the job; then that was her call to make.

Max Fortune didn't have to get everything he wanted, his way.

That thought turned out to be somewhat prophetic,

because early Monday morning—the day of their rescheduled shoot—he called her. He had to go to Kentucky for the day, a meeting over the horse deal. Unavoidable. Could they postpone?

"Given your short time frame," she said, thinking on her feet, "wouldn't it be better if I went ahead today? I'm sure Sky or one of her grooms could wrangle the horse."

Silence.

Delighted to have gained the ascendancy, she continued with calm confidence. "That's if you trust me to know what I'm doing with the camera…which I hope you do, since you engaged me, specifically, for this job."

Without his disturbing presence, the shoot had gone brilliantly. Once set loose in the field, his mare had pranced about and performed for the camera like a trouper. In fact, Diana had recognized so much of her mother in the horse's showmanship that she'd secretly nick-named her *Maggie*.

But her delight on the day was nothing compared to her excitement on seeing the results in print. She'd wanted to tear out to the estate and show them to Max then and there. But it was late and she wasn't certain he'd even returned from his trip. If he had, they could end up alone, side by side, leaning over a desk scattered with prints. Hands brushing as they both reached for their favorite. Eyes meeting as they acknowledged that shared moment.

Bad idea. Very bad idea.

So she'd sealed the proofs in an envelope which she'd given to Eliza to deliver. Then she'd spent the ensuing two days starting every time the phone rang or the door to the gallery opened. Being midweek in winter, that wasn't very often. His continued silence was gnawing at her patience.

This morning—Thursday—she'd called the stables and learned from Sky that he'd gone somewhere with Nash for the day. She wasn't sure where or when he'd be back. Diana left a message impressing her urgency. To deliver the finished prints tomorrow, she needed his order as soon as possible.

By midafternoon he still hadn't called. However Jeffrey had, from Rapid City where he was shooting a special commission over several days. Diana had been manning the fort at *Click* by working extra hours and, he hated to ask, but could she cope if he stayed an extra night?

After assuring him that she wasn't in danger of overwork since things were midwinter slow, he suggested she close the doors and go home ahead of the forecast snow.

"It has barely started to flurry," she protested.

"All the more reason to leave now. See you tomorrow, Diana. And thank you for being so adaptable with your hours. You are a treasure!"

A smattering of snowflakes drifted sporadically from the lowering sky as she finished locking up. Distracted by the weather and the prospect of a cold walk to the parking lot, she wasn't thinking about Max for the first time in several days. She dropped the keys into her tote bag and turned toward the street…and there he was, right there in front of her.

It was such a shock that she slipped on the wet stoop and might have landed ignominiously on her backside if he hadn't caught her elbow and stopped her slide.

"Steady," he murmured. "I've got you."

Yes, he did. By both arms and with her nose pressed close to his chest. When she inhaled, the sting of icy air was tempered by a combination of body-warmed wool and even warmer man. That didn't help her regain her equilibrium much.

Max, being Max, released her in his own good time. The big, capable hands that cupped her elbows slid the length of her forearms to her hands. A frown pinched his brow. "No gloves?"

"I left them somewhere." Hearing how lame that sounded, she winced. "In my car, I think."

"Is that where you're heading?"

"Yes, and then home."

Which sounded even lamer. Next she'd be telling him where she'd parked her car and why, and then they'd move on to the scintillating subject of the weather and why she'd shut the gallery early. Perhaps if she reclaimed her hands she might also reclaim the use of her brain....

"I'd given up on hearing from you today," she said. "Let me get my keys and I'll open up again."

"You're not worried about the weather? I don't want to hold you up now it's snowing."

"This isn't snowing," she told him. "And you're holding me up more by not letting go of my hands."

He didn't let her go. "Do you have coffee in there?"

"I have the makings."

"Let's go somewhere that has it already made."

Crowding even closer under the narrow awning that sheltered the gallery's entrance, he nodded toward the adjacent block. "How about that place?"

Heart sinking, Diana followed the direction of his gaze. "Alberto's is nice, but…"

Alberto had a fascination for Broadway musicals and had decorated accordingly. The last time she'd eaten there, Diana found herself seated beneath a huge poster of her mother. It had felt odd and uncomfortable, yet she didn't like drawing attention to her relationship with the famous Maggie Fielding. In Sioux Falls she enjoyed being plain old anonymous Diana Young. Not Maggie and Oliver Fielding's daughter. Not anyone's wife-on-display.

"But?" Max prompted. "Do they serve coffee?"

"Yes, but—"

"Is it warm?"

"Yes."

"Then why are we standing here freezing appendages off? Let's go."

Diana relaxed a smidge when she discovered that her mother's picture had been superseded by Hugh Jackman in white trousers and Hawaiian shirt, brandishing maracas. Alberto himself bustled over to take their coats and show them to a table. "This one," he said, choosing a table for two, "is warm and cozy."

But Max gestured to the row of diner-style booths along one wall. "We'll take one of those. We need the bigger table for business."

"You bring this lovely lady here to do business?" Alberto's gaze swept dramatically heavenward.

"And to warm her up," Max said. "It's snowing outside and she forgot her gloves."

"It's not snowing," she felt compelled to point out, for the second time. "It's barely a flurry."

Alberto scolded her over the gloves all the way to their table, but his dark eyes twinkled as Max slid into the booth alongside her instead of opposite. After taking their coffee orders, he handed them each a menu and waved aside their protestations. "You want to warm your lady, first you need to feed her. We can fix you a meal or perhaps one of Gia's delicious cakes? You decide while I make your coffee."

He left and Max leaned closer. An ironic smile tilted the corner of his mouth and lit his night-forest eyes. "Does our host have anything to do with your *buts?*"

Slightly lost in the effects of that smile, Diana frowned.

"Out in the street, when I suggested we come here."

Oh. Right. *Those* buts. "Alberto loves to play the role of authentic Italian host. You may have noticed his love of theatre."

"Hard not to. I doubt Eliza was responsible for this interior design."

In the process of looking around at the dramatic decor—posters and props and garish imitation sets—he managed to shift closer on the bench so their arms and shoulders brushed. So much for relaxation. So much for his crack about frozen appendages, too. The man radiated enough body heat that one second of fleeting contact warmed her from the tip of her long nose to her equally long toes.

As for his allegedly frozen bits…

Shielding her face behind the playbill-sized menu, she couldn't help glancing down. Just a brief peek at well-filled denim and the relaxed spread of his muscular thighs on the dark bench turned her slightly giddy. And very warm.

Bad move. Gigantic bad move.

"You want anything else?"

Diana blinked. And cautiously lowered her shield. She presumed he meant… "To eat?" She moistened her lips. "Are you eating?"

"I had a late lunch with Creed, so I'm good. But don't let that stop you."

She needed a few seconds to regain her composure, to rid herself of this hyper-sensitivity to his nearness, to attune herself to business. Meanwhile she studied the menu, and to her chagrin heard the low rumble of her empty stomach.

"Did *you* eat lunch?"

Under his questioning look, she sighed. "Not yet."

"No wonder you've lost weight."

"I've put on several pounds this winter," she retorted defensively, which only drew his gaze to her body. Contradictory warmth flushed through her, part response to his slow, lazy-eyed appraisal and part anger because she shouldn't have to defend her weight. She closed the menu purposefully. "I'm going to have the chocolate amoretti cake."

With finely-honed timing, Alberto arrived with their coffees and took her order. After he'd left, Diana signaled that it was time to get down to business by nodding at the package of photos he'd tossed on the table.

"Have you had a chance to look at the proofs?"

"Yes," he said. "They're good."

"You say that as if you're surprised."

"I am surprised you got everything so right on your first job."

Sky must have told him....

Diana felt the flush of color in her face, annoyance at being caught out and counter-annoyance for feeling that annoyance. It wasn't as though she'd lied to him. The question of her experience had never come up.

"My first *paid* job," she countered, angling her body in the narrow seat so she could meet his eyes. "The series I took at the Fortune estate, of Sky's horses and the barn and the big house, took months of hard work. If you'd cared to ask, I would have suggested you come down to the gallery to see the exhibit."

"They're on show?"

"At *Click*." And because he still looked dubious, she couldn't help adding, "Jeffrey chose to exhibit them over a lot of professionals."

His eyes narrowed. "Jeffrey your date at the wedding?"

"That's right. *Click* is his gallery and studio. Jeffrey also teaches classes, which is how I started in photography. He saw something he liked and took me under his wing."

"I bet he did."

Diana bristled at the implication in his mocking drawl. "You said yourself that my work is good. And now you're inferring that Jeffrey only took me on to, what, get me into bed?"

Her voice rose indignantly on the last phrase, because she could see in his expression that he did think this.

And the notion was offensive, to her and to Jeffrey, who had never treated her with anything but respect. They dined together regularly, they'd done the wedding semi-date, but he'd never tried anything. Not even a quick goodbye kiss. And Max dared to imply…

She had to pause her silent fuming when one of Alberto's daughters brought her dessert. Max charmed the girl with his Aussie accent and his smile, which didn't help Diana's mood much. When he ordered them each a second coffee without consulting her, that highhanded-ness added another element to her simmering pot of ire.

Struggling for composure, she picked up her spoon and cut through the multi-layers of cake and frosting and cream. But she couldn't bring it to her mouth. She was pretty sure the effort of swallowing would choke her. "Don't judge Jeffrey," she said tightly, "by your own standards."

"Are you suggesting that I gave you this job to get you into bed?"

"Why did you offer it to me? What made you do a complete about-face?"

"I told you. Sky had engaged your services—I shouldn't have made the work untenable. Also, I liked your vision of the photos you wanted to take of Booty, as an athlete."

He knew exactly what to say, the clever devil, but Diana remained wary of his flattery. "Is that all?"

"You said an apology wouldn't be enough. Do you remember?"

Of course she remembered. She'd told him it would take more than sorry to make up for his offensive comment about sharing her body. The memory still twisted tight and ugly in her stomach. "And you think this will do it?"

"I think it's a start."

A start toward what?

Diana's heart did a little bumpety-bump as she recalled how this had begun in the library with talk of his unfinished business. She remembered the breathless catch in her lungs as the punch of shock hit: *she* might very well be that business. And she reminded herself that it didn't matter because once he selected his prints and paid his account, the job was over.

"A start, yes," she said briskly, pushing her plate out of the way and reaching for the photos. "Now let's see which prints you want to order so we can finish."

Max let her go ahead and think that... for the time being. Meanwhile he turned his attention to selecting pictures. It wasn't a tough task. He'd decided on his favorites from a score of impressive shots the first time he opened the envelope. But he made a big deal of studying them all again because he enjoyed listening to her serious-voiced explanations and he enjoyed watching her eyes light with enthusiasm and he enjoyed the way her body started to relax next to his as she became engrossed in the subject.

On the other hand, he was very aware of the weather and couldn't stretch the process out for as long as he would have liked.

Leaving the restaurant he paused to squint at the sky. Enough snow had fallen to whiten the pavement and the lamps cast an eerie glow over the streetscape.

"Is *this* snowing?" he asked.

"Almost."

He heard the smile in her voice and felt the brush of body contact as she craned her neck to look past him. He also felt her deep-seated shiver as the wall of cold hit.

"Isn't it pretty?" Her voice held an abstracted note of wonder. "I wish I had my camera!"

"You're shivering too hard to hold it steady."

"No. I'm not."

Amused by her indignation, Max shook his head. "Come on. Let's get you to your car or Alberto will have my hide for not keeping you warm."

"I'm parked a couple of blocks—" she pointed off to their right "—down there."

"A couple of blocks?"

"It's not far."

"Speak for yourself, snow-babe." He hunched deeper into his jacket. "I'd have to walk it two ways."

"You don't have to walk me to my car."

He gave her a *yeah, I do* look and because he could feel her gathering resistance, took matters into his own hands. With an arm around her shoulder, he tucked her firmly into his side where she had always fit so well— the perfect height, the perfect shape, the perfect response purring through his blood. "I'm parked right here. I'll drive you that couple of blocks."

Ignoring whatever protest she muttered, he hurried her to the four-wheel drive Nash had loaned him for the duration of his visit and bustled her into the passenger seat. When she fumbled with the seat belt catch he took her hands in his and found them ice cold. He swore beneath his breath. "You're frozen already and you wanted to walk to your car?"

"Only my hands, which I would put in my pockets if you'd let them go."

She attempted to tug free of his grip but he held on a moment longer. "You've changed," he said quietly, looking into eyes that, but for their wariness, hadn't changed in ten years. "I don't remember you ever being this argumentative."

"I don't remember you ever being this domineering."

He laughed and shook his head. "I don't remember you having such a sharp mouth. You used to be softer. Quieter. More amenable."

"I used to be young. And if amenable is a euphemism for walkover, then I'm pleased to have changed. Now, if you really don't want me to freeze, I suggest you shut the door and turn on the heat."

Okay. She had a point. And while he chuckled quietly at her bossy tone, he followed instructions and soon the heater had cast a thick blanket of warmth over the vehicle's interior. The wipers were also doing their job, slapping a wet rhythm through the slushy snow. "Tell me you don't miss L.A. on days like this," he muttered, steering into the street.

"I don't."

"Not even the valet parking?"

"Give me Phillips Avenue over Rodeo Drive any day of the year!"

Max cut her a sideways look. "You're serious?"

She met his gaze with a steady directness. "The winter weather can get much worse than today but I don't mind. I'm not just saying that to be argumentative and it's not only because I'm happy here in Sioux Falls. It's true. I'm a winter person at heart. My best photographic work, the shots that people stop and *really* study in the gallery, are the ones in the winter collection. I've even come to enjoy the cold and—" She pointed left. "Turn here. That's me, right there."

She pointed out an SUV, a tradesmanlike model, not sporty, not luxury. "This one?"

She nodded. "My winter wheels."

He pulled in behind but left the engine—and heater—running. "And in summer you drive a…?"

"A bike."

"You drive a *motor*bike?"

Laughing softly, she shook her head. "Good grief, no. A bicycle. You probably haven't noticed but we have a blacktop bike path that follows the river all the way through town. I'm looking forward to riding to work when the weather warms up."

"I guess you didn't do much bike riding on Rodeo Drive."

"Sadly, no. They won't valet park bikes."

Despite the levity of her answer, her smile held a tinge of sadness that smacked Max hard. For the life of him he couldn't return the smile or find a single witty response. He recalled the night of Case's wedding, when he'd first learned of her unhappy marriage. She'd rerouted the conversation and he'd kidded himself that he didn't want to know about her marriage.

But that shadow of hurt in her eyes sat all kinds of wrong in Max's gut. So did her comment about not wanting to be a walkover. Although she'd unfastened her seat belt and picked up her bag, he stalled her with a hand on her arm.

He felt her stillness, her gathering tension, even before he asked, "If you were so unhappy, why did you stay?"

"I couldn't leave. It was…complicated."

"Complicated how? Financially?"

She nodded. Then drew an audible breath before turning to meet his gaze. "Look, I love my life here," she said, and her steady sincerity chased the shadows from her eyes. "I love my job and my house and this easygoing, unpretentious place that lets me be myself. It took a while for me to get to this point, but now I'm as happy as when…"

She stopped for a split second, and Max took a stab at what she'd stopped herself saying. "As happy as when we were together?"

"We weren't 'together'," she said.

Max frowned. "I seem to remember *together*. I can name you a dozen places we were *together* in my apartment alone. And what about the time we didn't make it back inside, when we—"

"That was sex," she interrupted.

But it wasn't the frankness of her comment or the flush of color climbing her throat that stopped him mid-sentence. It was the hand she placed over his to stop him detailing that night in the darkened shadows of the stairwell. It was the unexpected touch of her fingers and the resulting flare of heat in his blood.

"We had an awful lot of sex," she continued, "in an awful lot of places. You're right. But that didn't make us a couple. I'm sorry that I didn't understand the distinction back then. My only excuse is I was young and, as you pointed out so accurately, amenable."

"Are you implying I took advantage?"

"No. I'm trying to explain how I misinterpreted, that's all. There was no advantage taken. That chemistry we had was a powerful thing."

Between the impact of her touch and the softened warmth of her rueful expression, it took Max several seconds to digest her actual words. To realize that she'd just handed him the opening he'd been probing for, easier than he could have hoped for. Much sooner than he'd expected.

"This chemistry…" Without dropping her gaze, he turned his hand and laced their fingers in an intimate bond. "It's still there, isn't it?"

Gently he traced the junction of her wrist with his thumb. He felt the jump of her pulse, saw the fireflash of awareness in her eyes. And the wariness.

"Yes," she admitted finally. "But I'm not interested in doing anything about it."

"Why not? We're both single. Unattached. We both know how good we were together. We both remember that."

"I told you. I'm happy with my life. The last thing I want is a short-term affair or a one-night stand for old time's sake or whatever it is you have in mind. So you can forget about you and me, *together,* right now!"

"I'm not sure I can do that."

She stared back at him as if she couldn't quite believe what she'd heard. Then slowly, disbelievingly, she shook her head. "I'm not the girl I was ten years ago, Max. Nothing you say or do will change my mind. Really, I am just not interested."

Five

Surprisingly, Max didn't debate the issue or push her for any further explanation. He let her go with nothing but a parting suggestion to "find those gloves" and "stay warm," but Diana knew he would take her *not-interested, can't-change-my-mind* declaration as a challenge.

At first she'd kicked herself soundly for not realizing the pleasure a goal-oriented man like Max would take in overcoming such a clearly stated obstacle. But then she discovered a perverse satisfaction in having the suspicions she'd harbored ever since his turnabout at Case's wedding confirmed. Now she wouldn't have to second-think his every comment, every action, every touch.

Their mutual attraction was acknowledged. His desire to get her into bed was established. And she chose to treat it as a test, a chance to prove her strength of character.

He couldn't make her change her mind. Diana was confident—and energized—by her own goal to resist whatever temptation he placed in her path.

"I'm ready, Max Fortune." Dressed for work the next morning in winter-white cashmere that flattered her coloring, she fixed herself with a steady glare in the dresser mirror. "Bring on your worst."

The overnight snowfall wasn't as heavy as anticipated and Jeffrey arrived back in town half an hour after Diana opened the doors at *Click*. They caught up on business news and he looked over her proofs of the horse she'd christened Maggie. They debated some of her choices of composition, and his suggestion to crop one full-body shot back to head and superbly arched neck sparked excitement in her creative soul.

She set off to print Max's order with that bonus extra, all thoughts of seduction forgotten.

When she strode back into the gallery an hour later, her satisfied smile reflected a job well done. Jeffrey's comments had evoked several subtle changes and the enlarged prints looked even better than she'd envisioned. She couldn't wait to show them off.

Following the low murmur of Jeffrey's voice, she turned the corner in the L-shaped gallery and stopped short. Jeffrey and Max were studying *her* exhibit. The smile froze on her face, even as her heart lurched to life.

She hadn't expected to see him until late in the afternoon, when she'd suggested his prints would be ready to collect.

"Ah, there you are!"

It was Jeffrey who spoke, but her eyes were on Max as he turned. There was something in his expression, some slow burn of appreciation that caused her heart to beat faster, and she couldn't look away.

Then Jeffrey cleared his throat, loudly, and she realized how long the silence had stretched.

"You're early," she said hurriedly. "I've only just finished printing and there is still some—"

"I'm not here for my photos," he assured her. "I'm here to look at yours."

Oh.

"Max was particularly keen to see your winter compilation," Jeffrey said. "He has good taste."

And a good sense of which particular flattery might turn her head, Diana thought, recovering from her initial response to his presence. She'd invited him to do his worst and this, most likely, was it.

Knowing that he aimed to butter her up, that it was all a seduction ruse, would help her keep any complimentary observations he made in perspective.

With measured steps she approached the two men, her chary gaze sliding from Jeffrey's face to Max's and then on to the series of pictures she called her Gothics. The Fortune family's big estate house with its dark stone facade, its stark black-roofed angles and wrought iron gables, the imposing array of chimneys and lighthouse cupolas that jutted into the sky…all set against the stark white of a heavy Christmas snowfall.

Looking at the pictures always gave her a deep-seated chill, of satisfaction and because of the subject matter.

"Well?" she asked. "What do you think?"

"The truth?"

Diana hazarded a sideways glance and found him studying *her,* not the pictures. She ignored the little flutter in her pulse. "Of course I want to hear what you really think. Go ahead. Be brutal."

One eyebrow crooked, as though asking if she was sure, and she made a go-ahead gesture with her hand. He turned back to the pictures. "They're cold," he said without preamble. "No life, no color, no movement." His gaze flicked back to hers. "I gather that's the point?"

Jeffrey chuckled. "Exactly. You should feel the extremes of these in your bones. That *is* the point. Now, if you contrast those with the horse set—"

The phone began to ring, distracting Jeffrey's attention. "I'll get it," Diana said, already pivoting on the heels of her favorite cherry-red boots.

"No, no. You can clarify your motivations better than I. You stay."

For several seconds nothing broke the silence except the echo of Jeffrey's retreating footsteps. Diana pretended to study the pictures she knew by heart, waiting until he was out of earshot before ending this vignette and sending Max on his way.

"Cold getting to you?"

Frowning, she looked down and realized she was rubbing her hands together. Not that she was prepared to admit to nerves. She smiled wryly. "Proof positive that the pictures are effective."

His eyes remained on her hands a moment longer, reminding her of the previous day. The work-roughened texture of his big hands closing over hers, the intimate slide as their fingers laced together, the hot spark of awareness when he persuaded her to admit that she still felt this attraction.

"Did you find your gloves?"

"Not yet." Forcing those images from her mind, from her blood, she shrugged. "But I'm sure they will turn up somewhere."

He returned his attention to the exhibit, moving on to the collection featuring Sky's playful colts, giving her the moment's reprieve she needed. He pointed out a shot of two colts at full stretch gallop, racing each other across the field, neck to neck. It was a vibrant, lively, colorful contrast to the winter shots.

"I want this one."

Diana blinked, unsure if she'd heard him right. "You want to buy it?"

"That's right."

A warm pool of pleasure settled low in her tummy, even as she shook her head. "I'm sorry, but these are for exhibit only."

"They're not for sale? Why not?"

"They belong to Sky, actually. The whole family did me a big favor giving me free rein to shoot all over the estate. It wouldn't feel right to sell them. I don't have that right." Uncomfortable beneath the assessing intensity of his gaze, she hurried on. "Look, Max, there's no need to pretend interest or to buy my favors. It won't impress me or sway me."

"You think that's what I'm doing?"

"Isn't it?"

"You've turned into a cynic," he accused, although he looked almost amused by the discovery.

Diana didn't disagree. After yesterday's revelation, a combination of cynicism and suspicion seemed like the ideal attitude. "I have work to do. Is there anything else?"

"I'm having lunch with Nash and Patricia at the Fortune Hotel." One corner of his mouth kicked up into an appealing grin. "Why don't you join us?"

"I'd love to, but I have this work to finish. Important client. Prints promised for this afternoon. Sorry," she finished cheerfully, enjoying the perfect excuse a little more than necessary. It helped balance out the tingle in her blood caused by that grin and the disappointment in her stomach because her suspicions about his visit had been confirmed. It was a ruse, another attempt to woo her, when she craved genuine interest in her work. "I really do need to get back to work, so I'll leave you to your browsing."

"Before you go, I want to make one thing clear."

Diana had taken a dozen brisk steps but now she stopped. Eyebrows elevated in question, she turned back.

"I didn't book you for the photography job to get you into bed."

There was a directness in his gaze that gave her a moment's pause—perhaps he was sincere—but only a moment's. "I've done an excellent job on the photos," she told him. "I know you and your parents will be very happy with the results. Does it matter why you chose me?"

He closed down the space between them without breaking eye contact. Diana stood her ground despite the misgivings dancing all over her nerves.

"Yes, it matters," he said, stopping in front of her. "Come to lunch. Let me explain why. I'm sure this important client of yours will understand if his prints are late."

"I'm sorry, Max, but you'll have to do better than that."

Coolly, she turned and started to walk away. She felt his gaze tracking her every step but she maintained her composure. Even when he drawled his worrying rejoinder.

"Honey, I haven't even started yet."

Max strode into the foyer of the Fortune's Seven with his plan to do better already taking shape in his mind. He didn't have a lot of time and the days he'd wasted this week—days spent chasing the ownership of their second-choice stallion and all to no avail—added pressure to a situation that required patience and finesse. Enticing Diana to drop her guard would not be easy, but in that closing comment she'd issued a second challenge he couldn't refuse.

He would do better.

And he would prove to her that they'd had a lot more going for their relationship—in their *togetherness*—than just an *awful lot of sex*…even if it took an awful lot of sex to prove it!

Today was supposed to be a first step along that path. He'd hoped to cajole her into lunch with Nash and Patricia to prove he enjoyed and valued her company in places other than the bedroom—or darkened stairwell, for that matter. He figured she knew the Fortunes well enough to be at ease, that they'd all enjoy a nice, easy, family kind of togetherness.

He'd only met Nash and Patricia himself a couple of months back, when they'd visited Australia to meet their long-lost Fortune relatives. They'd spent time with the whole family at Crown Peak, then they'd traveled to his station to experience the true outback and it was like welcoming old family into his home. Perhaps because they had so much in common with his parents, the same strong bond of friendship that cemented their marriage, the kind he'd set his mind on finding for himself because nothing less would cut it.

Max thought he'd found his partner in Diana…but only after she'd shaken him up by questioning their relationship and her reason for staying. Only after she'd turned his world on its ear by leaving so abruptly. Only after he'd missed her so intensely that he knew he'd found his life-mate when he'd least expected it.

"Max."

Nash's greeting halted his stride and his deep reflection. He turned to find the man he'd come to think of as an uncle—and a favorite one, at that—had followed him into the hotel. He was alone.

"Patricia couldn't make it," Nash explained, reading the question in Max's expression. His handshake was as strong as always but a frown creased his forehead and clouded his usually sharp blue eyes.

"Is everything all right?"

"I wish I could answer that." Nash raked a hand through his thick dark hair. Although marginally into his sixties, he could pass for ten years younger…except for now when worry etched hard lines into his still-handsome face. "In all honesty, I don't know. Lately she's been…not herself."

"Health issues?" Max asked.

"She says there's nothing wrong, that I'm imagining things." He made a rueful sound. "Maybe she's right, but I do know she works too hard and spends all her energy looking after everyone else but herself. I can't help but worry that the next strong wind will blow her all the way to Alaska. Hell, she needed this lunch a darn sight more than either of us!"

"She might still be recovering from your trip," Max suggested, looking for some form of reassurance. "Those long flights to and from Australia can knock a person around, especially when she's not used to air travel."

"You might have a point. Whatever the reason, Patricia's not here and—" he looked around "—I don't see your guest, either…"

"Diana couldn't get away from work."

Max had mentioned bringing someone to lunch, but identifying that guest as Eliza's friend cleared some of the distraction from Nash's gaze. "Ah, Diana. I hadn't realized you two were old friends."

Friends? Max was pretty sure Diana wouldn't approve that term, but he let it slide. "I hadn't realized you knew about our relationship."

"I overheard Eliza and Patricia talking at breakfast. I didn't pay a lot of attention, but I did hear that you and Diana met in Australia."

"Ten years ago."

"Just friends?" Nash asked. "If you don't mind me asking."

"I don't mind," Max replied easily. "We were never just friends."

"Would Diana be the reason you decided to stay on a while longer?"

"One of them. Although let's not discount your hospitability."

Nash snorted. "Save your sweet talk for the lady. She might buy it."

She might. Although Max wasn't counting on it. He knew it was going to take more than talk, no matter how sweet, to woo the new, changed, less amenable, more cynical Diana. "I'll let you know how that works out," he said dryly. "And speaking of buying, I visited *Click* on my way here and saw the photos Diana took out at the estate."

"Do you like them?"

"Enough that I'm keen to buy several, but Diana believes they're not hers to sell. What do you think, Nash? Any chance I can procure a couple to take home with me as souvenirs?"

Diana didn't have to wait long to discover what Max had meant by *honey, I haven't even started yet.* The first gift arrived at *Click* the morning after his visit to the gallery, hand-delivered by a junior from one of the boutiques located in the Fortune's Seven shopping arcade. She'd wanted to send whatever it was straight back, but that would have put the teenaged employee in a tricky middleman position.

Diana couldn't do that. She would send it back to Max herself.

The prettily embossed cream-and-gold box sat untouched for all of thirty minutes before inquisitiveness got the better of her. What could it be? What would he have sent? What would he have chosen? When she picked it up and weighed it in her hands, curiosity sang an *open-me open-me* siren's chant.

"Oh, for goodness sake," she admonished, rolling her eyes at herself. "It won't hurt to take a peek."

It wasn't as if she'd be tempted to keep the contents, not when David's propensity to buy gifts for all the wrong reasons—for show, as bribes, to atone for bad behavior—had replaced her pleasure in receiving pretty things with cynicism. That voice of cynicism whispered that Max wouldn't have even chosen the gift. More likely he'd called someone at Dakota Fortune—someone like Sasha Kilgore, the PR assistant Creed dated—and asked her to do the choosing.

That thought helped distance her from any silly romantic notions…until she lifted the lid of the box and found a pair of fluffy-lined suede gloves nestled inside. Then it didn't matter who'd done the actual choosing because only Max could have come up with the idea. She couldn't do a darn thing to halt the warm smile of pleasure that started somewhere deep inside and quickly danced through her whole body. Her hands were shaking slightly as she opened the tiny gift card. The inscription was in his handwriting, just three words that made her laugh out loud.

NOW I've started.

On Sunday it was coffee and two of her favorite glazed donuts, delivered to her home in time for breakfast. On Monday, a miniature book of quotations themed around winter waited at the gallery when she arrived for work. On Tuesday, nothing, and she had to give herself a stern talking to for suffering an extreme sense of letdown.

She knew he was spending the day in Deadwood, visiting Blake Fortune's casinos. She knew because he'd called the night before and invited her to go with him. Of course she'd said no and then she'd told him to stop sending gifts and he'd asked if she liked his choices so far and she'd been unable to straight-out lie.

"I'm collecting them all for charity," she told him primly. "The Sioux Falls Children's Center thanks you."

He laughed and said if he'd known he would have sent enough donuts for all the kids and multiple copies of the latest Harry Potter instead of the book of quotations. Darn him. Not only did he choose the perfect gifts for a gift cynic, but now he was managing to charm her with the perfect responses!

She'd gone to sleep with his soft laughter curling through her blood.

Her dreams had been very, very sweet.

With Max out of town, Tuesday crawled by in apprehensive anticipation. So far his gifts had been unique, carefully considered, fun. She'd enjoyed the little thrills of excitement, wondering what each new day would bring.

Not that she'd forgotten that he was using the gifts to try and charm her out of her pants. But since she did know and since she had no intention of succumbing, where was the harm in enjoying the game? For the first time in years she felt sexy and, yes, flattered by the attention.

But Wednesday was Valentine's Day and she hadn't realized the full potency of his guerilla gift-giving campaign until the roses arrived shortly before she left for work. Two dozen deep red hothouse blooms. Her sense of letdown was immense, a tummy-churning eddy of disappointment, not only because he'd succumbed to sending the traditional romantic fare but because he knew about her aversion to roses.

He'd *known,* she corrected herself.

Ten years ago he'd known because she'd shared the reason in a game of bedroom truth-or-dare that had taken a sudden turn from sexy fun into emotional intimacy. She'd told him that roses had been her mother's signature bloom, an arrangement in every room, their scent an omnipresent memory of her childhood. And after Maggie's death they'd been inundated with sheaf after sheaf, until their home was fit to explode from the overpowering fragrance. Diana had never wanted to see or smell another rose for as long as she lived.

Max forgetting that long-ago disclosure shouldn't have created such bitter disappointment, but it did. She dealt with it by dumping the flowers—and the unopened card— in the trash. Then she washed any trace of their fragrance from her hands and set off to work fired with angry resolve.

The game was over.

Another delivery arrived while she was in the studio working on digital retouching. This was an area she still needed to practice and refine before she could call herself an expert. At the moment she was competent but that wasn't good enough. After several concentrated hours she needed a break. And lunch. She wandered into the office to fetch her purse and found the gift bag sitting on her desk.

Her early-morning spike of disappointment about the roses had leveled out into pragmatic relief. She'd needed that wake-up-to-yourself slap. She'd needed the reminder of how easy it would be to fall for Max Fortune all over again.

"Aren't you going to open it?"

She swung around from her contemplation of the gift bag and found Jeffrey in the doorway, watching her closely. She looked from him to her desk with a sinking feeling in the pit of her stomach. *Oh, please, no, don't let this be an overture from Jeffrey.*

"I was wondering if there's been a mistake," she said, wording her message with careful tact. "If perhaps this has been delivered to the wrong person? I'm not a fan of Valentine's Day, you see. My ex cured me of that sentiment."

Jeffrey winced. "Well, I'm starting to feel like an ass!"

"Oh, please, don't," she said quickly.

"Too late now." He shrugged with apparent good humor. "Have you read my card?"

"Not yet."

"I thought as much, seeing as you've said not a word. But I think you'll like that part of my gift, at least. We can discuss over dinner."

He left her then, alone with her unwanted gift and a card he thought she'd like and a reminder that their regular dinner nondate was tonight. In her absorption with Max and his dashed gifts, she'd completely forgotten. Annoyed with herself and with Jeffrey, with Max, with her mother and everyone who'd ever sent her roses, and with herself again for all this angst, she sat down and ripped open the tissue-wrapped box she found nestled inside the gift bag.

"Oh, dear Lord."

Stunned, she slumped back in her chair. It was a charm bracelet and she knew without opening the attached card that this wasn't from Jeffrey. A dozen wildly conflicting emotions duked it out in her stomach and chest and head as she lifted the bracelet and turned it over in her shaky hands.

Not the same one as he'd bought her all those years ago when it had caught her eye as they strolled past a Sydney market stall, but an expensive designer model she recognized by its *Woo-Me* charms. She couldn't help being moved by his choice and charmed by the message, and at the same time confounded by how he'd gotten this so right and the roses so woefully wrong.

She didn't want it to matter this much and the fact that it did confirmed her decision. She'd been enjoying this attention a little too much, flirting with the dangerous allure of being wanted again by Max. But it was getting out of hand and now was the time to call a halt while she still had the strength and commitment to say no.

Without giving herself a chance to think it through and possibly change her mind, Diana reached for the phone and dialed the number of Sky's horse stud office.

Max was waiting on a call from Kentucky about the stallion he and Zack had selected as their number one choice for the new stud farm. Finally the ownership syndicate had agreed to negotiate on terms. There was still a ways to go, some final obstacles to overcome, but at least he could see the finish line.

He picked up on the second ring and the cool silken clip of Diana's phone-voice wiped all thoughts of business from his mind. He'd been expecting this call, too, and a smile curved his lips as he settled back in Sky's comfy office chair to enjoy the exchange.

"Good," he said without preliminaries. "You got my gift."

"Both of them."

What? Max frowned. "I'm talking about the bracelet."

"I got that. And the roses."

"Roses? Why would I send you roses?" That wasn't something he'd forget, the fact she loathed them or the reason behind it. "From what I remember, you'd feed them straight into the garbage disposal."

"Yes," she said quietly, and Max could hear the puzzlement in her voice.

He sat up straighter, focusing on the fact that she had got flowers. And not from him. "I guess you have another admirer. My money is on your boss," he mused, not liking it in particular, but preferring it was the innocuous Jeffrey to anyone else. "Although I thought he'd know you better."

"Why do you say that?"

"I thought he'd know about your aversion to roses."

"I didn't mean his choice of gift. Why would you think he'd send me flowers? Why would you call him an 'admirer.' We don't have that kind of relationship."

No, they didn't. He'd noticed at the wedding. But she sounded so put out, so genuinely confounded, that he couldn't help teasing. "Honey, I listened to him wax lyrical about you for ten minutes straight the day I came to the gallery. He is a big admirer."

"Of my work."

He chuckled at her quick defense. Hell, he could hear her raised hackles right through the phone and he was preparing the words to smooth them right back down with the long, slow verbal caress of his own admiration, when he noticed the second call coming in. Kentucky, curse the timing. Although, on second thoughts, he'd as soon do the stroking in person. Tonight.

"Honey, I have another call I have to take. It looks like we might have some action on the horse deal at last. I'll tell you about it tonight. Is eight good for you?"

There was a beat of silence. "Good…for what?"

"For dinner. I assume that's why you called. As per instructions."

"What do you—"

"Listen, I have to go. I will pick you up ten before eight. Oh, and you might want to wear your dancing shoes."

"Wait just a second," she said sharply, before he could end the call. "I can't do that. I already have a date for tonight."

"Then break it."

"Why in heaven's name would I want to do that?"

"Because if the call I'm about to take goes to plan, this may be my last night in Sioux Falls. I want to spend it with you, Diana."

Six

Diana picked up the gift card from her desk and opened it, her hands not quite steady. *This may be my last night in SF. Dinner? Call me.* Beneath he'd printed the number she had just called.

No wonder they'd been at cross purposes. He'd assumed she'd read the card and he was expecting her to call. *As per instructions.* She shook her head, recalling all he'd said and the assumptions he'd made.

I will pick you up. She didn't think she'd imagined the emphasis on *will*.

Wear dancing shoes.

Break your date.

That had left her bristling with indignation over what she'd thought to be his highhandedness…until he'd taken her breath with the simple sincerity of that last line.

I want to spend it with you, Diana.

Temptation drummed hard and fast through her veins as she picked up the bracelet and played the charms through her fingers. It was a beautiful piece, so suggestive of their past relationship, such a perfect symbol of his present campaign. The little charms said "woo-me" but the subtext was about something far more earthy than wooing.

This last week, his attention, their repartee, her success in standing up for herself in spite of temptation, had left her feeling sexy and confident and good about herself. Sleeping with Max had always made her feel *very* good about herself. Perhaps she should just go ahead and indulge herself. It wasn't as though she hadn't thought about it—or fantasized about it— many times in the past week.

It wasn't as though she had anything stopping her… nothing, that is, except the fear she would want more than he was offering. Again.

Except did she want more this time around?

Didn't she have all that she wanted, here in the new life she'd constructed for herself in Sioux Falls?

Perhaps she should dine with him, dance with him, and shine as the woman he made her feel when she was with him. Not the disappointing daughter or the trophy wife, but a desirable woman. That's how Max had always made her feel…when he wasn't causing her to grind her teeth in frustration at his domineering my-way-or-the-highway approach.

Perhaps she should go to dinner with him and, instead of over-thinking, see how the night panned out.

Except she hadn't been joking about another date—

although usually she didn't refer to the Wednesday nights she and Jeffrey ate together as dates. They were more a sharing of food and company, a chance to talk about work away from the work environment. Mostly they ate out, but since she'd taken a series of culinary classes—one of the many practical skills she'd pledged to master in her quest for an independent, everywoman life—Diana sometimes chose to cook for them.

Tonight happened to be one of those nights. She'd planned the menu and bought the ingredients, but did she want to go ahead? She closed her eyes and pressed her fingers against the lids. Jeffrey had sent the roses— that's what he'd been alluding to earlier when he'd called himself an ass. Damn, but this was awkward. She didn't want to ruin their professional relationship or their friendship. She would have to talk to him, to let him know she didn't welcome any romantic overtures.

As for the meal…

Perhaps she should go ahead and cook as planned, but for Max. A rueful smile curved her lips as she imagined the look on his face when he turned up at her door at ten before eight, as planned, to take her to dinner. Only to find his meal of French onion soup, followed by Peppery Filet Mignon with Hasselbaak potatoes and mixed baby greens, finished with Raspberry Crème Brûlée, all prepared and ready to serve. By Diana, who'd not known how to flip an egg or grill a steak or bake even a packet mixture cake ten years ago.

Now that would set him back on his heels!

Her heart beat faster as she anticipated his appreciation of the dinner, the setting, the fire she would build, the dress she would wear…the dress he might strip from her body beside that open fire…

If she chose to let him.

It may be his last night in Sioux Falls and he would spend at least part of it with her. They would eat, they might even dance, and then she would make up her mind about the rest.

Her conversation with Jeffrey turned out to be much easier than expected. The roses, apparently, weren't a romantic overture but a business one. In fact Jeffrey looked quite appalled at the misunderstanding.

Much relieved, Diana laughed it off. "Forget I even brought it up—it's been my day of crossed purposes. I really must start reading the cards before I open the gifts!" It was another bad habit she'd picked up during her years with David. Another she needed to shed. "Now, tell me about this business venture. You have me intrigued."

"I've mentioned the possibility of expanding before—"

Diana clapped her hands and grinned. "You're doing it? You're opening the second gallery? Where? In Rapid City?"

"Nothing's definite yet, but I'll fill you in on the plans tonight."

"About tonight…" She winced apologetically. "Would you mind if we postpone? It's just…something else has come up."

"A real date?"

"Sort of."

NO POSTAGE
NECESSARY
IF MAILED
IN THE
UNITED STATES

BUSINESS REPLY MAIL
FIRST-CLASS MAIL   PERMIT NO. 717-003   BUFFALO, NY

POSTAGE WILL BE PAID BY ADDRESSEE

SILHOUETTE READER SERVICE
3010 WALDEN AVE
PO BOX 1867
BUFFALO NY 14240-9952

"With the sender of gifts?" Curiosity danced across his expression and Diana gave herself a sharp kick for starting the dance tune. She knew he was naturally nosy—heck, he was the only man she knew who opened his newspaper to the page-six gossip column before the sports!

"Look, it's still a bit undecided," she said, not wanting to divulge names. Not wanting to talk about something she wasn't sure about herself. "We can talk about it next week."

"Sure," he said, but he looked as disappointed as a child denied a treat. "Why don't you take tomorrow off. In case you want to recover." He cocked an eyebrow. "Or sleep in."

"That won't be necessary."

He laughed at her prim answer. Or possibly at the flush of color climbing her cheeks. "Go on. Make it a long weekend, have fun, indulge yourself. But first you better go home and put those roses in water. They cost me an arm and half a leg. Oh, and don't forget to read the card."

Diana didn't have the heart to mention that she'd trashed both the roses and the card. That could wait until next week. Relieved that things were still good between them, she offered up a quick hug and fled before he asked any further questions about her date.

Diana's home sat at the bottom of a cul-de-sac, secluded from its neighbors by the spread of a generous yard thick with mature trees. Despite their size the gardens were well lit in the evening dark, as was the compact Mediterranean-style house at their heart. In fact the only *non*-neat thing Max had seen driving through the neighborhood was the untidily parked vehicle blocking the entrance to Diana's drive.

He paused to frown at the unprepossessing white sedan. It didn't look like the sort of vehicle a show pony like Jeffrey Lloyd would drive. And yet according to Eliza, he was "the date" for tonight, the one Diana had cited on the phone.

That telephone conversation had fired his confidence that her resistance was crumbling. He'd been certain she'd invented a convenient "date" as a last-gasp scrambling defense. But then he recalled the flowers she'd received—the ones she'd assumed were from him and which he'd assumed were from her boss.

What if he was wrong? What if she had a real date?

The prospect had cooled his confidence for a minute. He didn't relish looking the fool so when he bumped into Eliza late in the afternoon he coerced her into revealing that Diana did have a long-standing dinner engagement with her boss. *Every* other Wednesday night.

Tonight's "date" wasn't special. It was just a regular get-together which happened to fall on Valentine's Day and which happened to put a serious dent in Max's plans. Lucky he was adaptable…although he had counted on finding Diana alone.

His gaze glanced off the car to the iron-gated courtyard that protected the front entrance to the house. It wasn't yet six-thirty which seemed early for a dinner date. Maybe the car didn't belong to her date….

As he started down the path he caught the faint strum of music from inside the house, yet a sense of something-not-right niggled at his gut. Halfway through opening the gate, he heard the splintered sound of a glass or plate shattering. A male voice raised in anger chilled him to the bone and he set sail for the portico at a flat-out run.

The front door lay open. Not that it mattered. Max would have plowed right through the thick oak barrier to get to whatever was going on inside.

"Diana?"

She didn't answer. She didn't have to. He found her before he finished yelling her name, backed into a corner of the kitchen by the intruder.

Max wrapped a hand around the guy's puny arm and hauled him out of her face. He would have planted his other hand in the bastard's face if she hadn't stopped him.

"No. Max, don't! Let him go."

It wasn't her appeal that stopped him as much as her calm, imperative tone. He didn't release his grip on Jerkface but he did allow his gaze to slide to Diana's face for the first time since bursting into the room. She didn't look hurt or cowed. Although her face was pale and her eyes bright, he realized with a jolt that it wasn't fear. It was fury.

She confirmed this by telling him through tight lips to, "Throw him out if you want, but take care how you handle him."

"You know him?"

She nodded. "He's one of David's sons."

Easing his grip a fraction, Max took a second look at the intruder's face. Not an overwrought adolescent but older, at least midtwenties, with designer stubble and a belligerent expression that would have done any teenager proud. "You don't want me to hurt him, then?"

"Personally, I'd love you to hurt him. But then he would file an assault charge against you and he isn't worth the trouble."

The stepson spat out a short instructive response that sorely tempted Max's restraint. "You might want to watch your language," he suggested. "After you apologize to the lady."

"Lady? She's no lady. She's a cheating bit—"

Max could move quickly when he had to. His arm across the creep's chest turned the rest of his insult into a choking wheeze. "What do you want me to do with him?" he asked Diana.

"If you could see him off my property, that would be a help."

"Should he be on the road in his state?"

"He's not wasted," she said with a confidence that suggested she'd seen him when he was. "He'll be okay when he cools down."

Max returned to find Diana on her hands and knees sweeping up broken crockery from the tiled floor. But when he hunkered down beside her with a warning about the fine shards, she gave him a quelling look. "There is no need to point out the obvious."

"Like, what were you doing opening the door to your potty-mouthed stepson? That kind of obvious?"

She pushed to her feet and rubbed her hands down the front of her sweatpants. For the first time he noticed her casual attire. Not dressed up for a date or even for company. But then she lifted a hand to push a loose strand of hair from her face and he saw that it was trembling.

Delayed shock. And he'd jumped on her for letting the creep inside. He should thump himself for being a jerk.

"I didn't mean—"

"What did he say—"

They'd both spoken at once, and Max gestured for her to carry on. His apology could wait. He'd just add it to the growing list.

"Gregg—that's his name, for what it's worth—" She moistened her lips. "What did he say to you on the way out?"

"Nothing that bears repeating."

"If it concerns me, I would like to know."

Their gazes met and held, hers steady and unflinching despite that tremor in her hand. It struck him again how much she had changed, how strong she had grown, and how much he wanted to know this woman she'd become. This seemed like a place to start. "He suggested I was your latest lover, living the high life on his money. I gather by that he means his father's?"

"Yes. David left Gregg and his brother's inheritance in a trust setup, so they wouldn't go through it all in a couple of wild years. Gregg doesn't believe he has enough money to fund his Beverly Hills lifestyle."

"So he came here to hassle you for money?"

"That's what he does best." She sighed and slumped back against the island at her back. "Sometimes I think it would be easier if I just gave in and let him have what he wanted."

"Yeah, but you don't like giving in easily," he said softly. "Do you?"

It took a moment, a moment when she blinked and refocused on his face. Then she smiled and her smile grew to laughter that sounded like a release of pressure and pent-up anxiety. Still smiling, she narrowed her eyes at him. "You never miss an opportunity, do you?"

Max hitched a shoulder. "You've got to admit I have my uses."

"You do." The smile lingered on her lips, but in her eyes he saw a new awareness along with genuine gratitude. "Thank you. You arrived just in time. I was starting to worry that he'd go through all my dishes."

Although offered blithely, her quip reminded Max of the moment at the gate when he'd heard the brittle smash. He remembered the cold slice of fear and he couldn't return her smile. "Has he ever hurt you?" he asked.

"Physically? No. He's just obnoxious and insulting and prone to temper tantrums."

"Sounds like he needs pulling into line."

"Oh, I think it's way too late for that."

"No," Max said with conviction. "You can't let him get away with thinking he can intimidate you in your own home, whenever he needs some extra cash. One day he will go too far and I won't be here to intercede."

He watched her smile crumple at the edges but this time he didn't berate himself for unnerving her. Curse it, she needed to be more conscious of her vulnerability. And although he'd given the little punk a warning about what he'd do if he ever found him within a hundred yards of Diana again, it wasn't enough. He wouldn't be here the next time.

"I should have called the police," he said tightly.

"On what grounds? Gregg didn't exactly break in."

"How, exactly, did he get in?"

From her expression he knew he wouldn't like the answer. "He forced his way past me."

"You opened the door to him?"

"I didn't know it was him, for heaven's sake. I was cooking and I didn't look at the clock. I opened the door because I thought it was you!"

Max had been building to a slow simmer over her lack of security sense, frustrated by the knowledge that he wouldn't be here the next time Gregg came calling. That he couldn't keep her safe. It took an extra second for her words to register and by then she'd swung away from her position at the kitchen island. Seemingly to attend to something on the adjacent bench.

She'd been cooking? And expecting him? Puzzled, Max shook his head.

"Why are you here so early?" she asked. "I thought you said eight."

"I thought you had a date. I wanted to catch you before he arrived."

"I begged off. Why did you want to catch me?"

"To say goodbye."

She looked up sharply, something indefinable in her eyes. "So, you are going home?"

"If everything goes to plan in Kentucky tomorrow, yes."

"Oh."

He watched her fuss with some vegetables. She had quite the collection there, half-prepared. All she seemed to be doing right now was rearranging them, but she appeared to have far too many for one. "Who are you cooking for?" he asked.

"For you," she replied, not quite meeting his eyes. "I decided to surprise you. Instead of going out to dinner, I thought we could eat here. If that's all right with you."

She'd surprised him all right, but Diana didn't derive the satisfaction she'd envisaged when she'd come up with the ploy. In her imagined scenario the meal was cooked and the table set and aglow with candles when she glided to the door to welcome him. In her imagination she'd looked cool and calm and capable. She was wearing sleek black silk, not gray yoga pants. Stray tendrils of hair weren't stuck to her steamed face as she tried to balance the intricacies of preparing four dishes with the distraction of a large, charismatic man watching her every move.

Although on his best behavior, Max took up too much space, he passed comment on her cooking methods—she'd forgotten how skilled he was in the kitchen—and he kept refilling her wine glass.

"No more," she said, snatching her glass from his reach. "I've had enough."

"You don't have to drive anywhere," he pointed out.

No, but she did have to keep her wits about her. The incident with Gregg had shaken her up more than she'd let on, leaving her especially susceptible to Max's charms. Not to mention his gallant white-knight-on-a-charger rescue.

She hadn't made up her mind yet on how the night should end. But if she did take him to her bed, she wanted that decision cast in strength and confidence, not because of the vulnerabilities exposed by Gregg's intrusion.

That's why she'd settled on dinner at home, not only to surprise him with her skills but so she would control the evening's progress. If he managed to sneak in any more *pinot noir* refills, she could kiss control goodbye!

"Success," she said brightly, straightening from her zillionth oven inspection. "The potatoes are finally ready. We can eat!"

His early arrival had thrown her plans and her timing into turmoil. She'd not had time to change her clothes. She hadn't even considered setting the dining-room table with good crockery and candles, not with Max watching. So they ate informally in her small breakfast nook which Max rendered even smaller by virtue of his presence. Not that he was a big *big* man, just everything about him had a larger-than-life impact on her, especially at such close quarters. The accidental brush of their knees when he rose to remove their dishes. The unconscious play of his thumb against the coffee cup cradled in one large hand. The dark hair revealed by folded-back shirt cuffs on his strongly muscled forearms.

And while she was powerfully aware of him, of their aloneness, of the appreciation in his gaze as he watched her work and talk and eat, this was not the studied seduction she'd expected from Max. There'd been no mention of the gifts. After a phone call to cancel the restaurant booking, there'd been no further mention of what he had planned for the night.

Instead he'd kept a relaxed conversation rolling through dinner. They'd talked a lot about his weeks in America, the plans he and Zack had in place for their showplace stud on New Zealand's South Island, about the stallion they coveted and the syndicate of owners whose members were divided on whether to do business.

"We put a shuttle deal on the table which might suit them better than an outright sale," he said.

Diana frowned. "A shuttle deal?"

"Spring is the breeding season, when mares are bred and the boys are kept very busy earning their keep."

"And what do the boys do for the rest of the year?" she asked.

"Cool their heels waiting for next spring to roll around."

"What a waste."

"That's where the shuttle idea comes in, moving them between the northern and southern hemispheres."

"Ahh," she murmured, catching on. "So a stallion can get in two springs a year. Say, one in Kentucky and one in New Zealand."

"If he's lucky. Yeah."

Something in his expression and his voice—a lingering depth to that *yeah*—reminded Diana they were discussing sex. The business of reproductive sex, sure, but the next silent seconds seemed to stretch with a new tension. With the business of getting lucky. She felt the tingly warmth of it in her toes, felt the slow climb through her legs and the languid heaviness low in her body. And she couldn't meet his eyes. She wasn't ready for this moment.

She wasn't ready for decisions.

To cover her discomfiture, she packed their dessert plates and unused utensils. "So, that's why you're going to Kentucky tomorrow? To arrange for this shuttle deal?"

"We have some management issues to iron out, but that's the plan. I'm meeting with several of the key syndicate members."

"And once you've thrashed out the details, then you're going home?"

He didn't answer right away. She had to look up, to meet his eyes. And what she saw there—the strong burn of desire and determination—caught her breath. She knew in that instant that she'd been fooling herself about his intentions here tonight. While she cooked and all through dinner he'd been biding his time, waiting for this moment.

Hands flat on the table, she started to stand, to escape. He stopped her with a hand over hers. "Come with me. To Lexington."

"I have to work."

"Don't you ever take time off?"

She'd answered automatically, forgetting the extra day off Jeffrey had granted her just a few hours earlier. *To have fun. To indulge herself.* In her heart she felt the hard beat of enticement. She could do this. She could have a day, a night, perhaps a whole weekend of Max. Not here in her home, where the memories would linger. Nowhere near the curious eyes of her boss and her best friend.

No one would even need to know....

His hand moved on hers, a shift in pressure and then

the stroke of his thumb across the span of her wrist. A hint of a frown pulled at the bridge of his nose. "You're not wearing the bracelet."

"I…no." She shook her head. "I'm not keeping it."

His thumb stilled. "You don't like it?"

"Of course I like it." She laughed softly, wryly, as she shook her head. "You knew I'd love it the same as I loved the first one you bought me in Sydney. That's why you chose it."

"But you won't accept it?"

"Wouldn't that be accepting its purpose?"

"Which is?"

She sighed. "Can we stop playing this game? Please? It was fun at first, I admit, and you have a gift for finding the right gift."

"But?"

"You can't buy my favors or my forgiveness or anything else." Her eyes met his across the table, forestalling his protest with their serious expression. "My husband believed he could buy his way into or out of any tight spot with the right gift or check. It's taken some of the gloss off the process."

"Your husband sounds as charming as his son."

"You know the saying, like father, like—"

"Why did you marry him?"

This time she didn't mind the question or its abrupt edge that cut across the rest of her blithe comment. It wasn't the time for cynical comments. It was the time for honest talk, to clear up some misconceptions, to move beyond the past so they could concentrate on the now.

She met his eyes across the table, across the remains

of their meal, and gave the most honest answer she could find. It was also the truth.

"Because I had to."

Seven

Because I had to.

The phrase conjured up one instant, obvious reason and it reverberated through Max's mind in a gathering storm of shock and disbelief. "You were *pregnant?*"

"No." Then her eyes widened, as if the full impact of his meaning had suddenly taken hold. "*No.* I would never have married David if I'd been pregnant with your child! I can't believe you would think that...that you'd think I would keep a secret like that from you."

"You said you had to get married," he justified. "What else was I supposed to think?"

"There are other reasons."

"Such as?"

"Duty. Obligation. Business." He could see her tension, could feel its restlessness in the hand beneath his. She pulled it away and jumped to her feet. "Go ahead into the living room. I'll make more coffee."

Max followed her into the kitchen. "We don't need more coffee. Tell me what happened."

With a sigh she leaned back against the counter, as if she needed its support. "I don't know if you remember much of what I told you about my family, my father in particular."

"He was a big-shot director. Broadway plays. A couple of movies."

She nodded. "David started out as a financier, a backer for some of my father's plays. They struck up a business friendship—for want of a better word—and produced a couple of shows in partnership. David was the one who coerced Father into the movie business, which turned out to be a colossal blunder. To cut a long story short, my father got into financial trouble through his involvement in a couple of big-budget flops and David bailed him out."

Max had pretended to relax against the kitchen island but now he had a new tension in his gut. "Go on."

"It turned out that David put a price on repaying that substantial debt. He hated being a peripheral player in show business society. He wanted to be at the center of the in-crowd and that wasn't happening quickly enough for him. He saw this as a golden opportunity to jump-start his social status."

"By marrying you."

Surprisingly she didn't confirm the obvious. There was more, and Max could tell by the wounded shadows in her eyes that he was going to hate the more. Already he was wishing he had laid out the stepson, since it was too late to do the same to his father.

"He didn't want to marry me. He wanted to marry the Fielding name," she divulged in the same even tone with which she'd started. Almost as if she was reciting her lines. Practiced, poised, emotionless. "His first choice was my sister Rose."

"The actress?"

Although hardly a star, he'd noticed the Rose Fielding name. He noticed because of Diana and the family resemblance.

"Yes." Her smile held a bleak edge. "David saw her potential for stardom as an extra bonus."

"What happened?"

"All those phone messages from home, those last weeks I was in Australia? I thought it was another of my family melodramas but Rose really did need my help. You see, she'd had an affair with a big-name star. A *married* big-name star. David found out and he was using this knowledge, and Rose's guilty conscience, to pressure her into marriage."

"He was blackmailing her?" The tension that had been building inside Max exploded. "Why the hell didn't she go to the police?"

"With what? He wasn't exactly sending her written demands. I don't even know if he had any hard evidence of her affair, but that doesn't matter. He could have ruined her career with a few careless whispers in the right ears. Oh, and he threatened to tell Father, which was almost as bad!"

"Perhaps she should have thought of that before she got it on with her married co-star," he said curtly.

"Perhaps, but that's the thing with Rose. She doesn't think, she just *does*. And when she couldn't reach me, she took a cocktail of drugs and alcohol and went to bed."

No longer quiet and detached, her voice broke on those last three despairing words. Her eyes bore the sheen of unshed tears and something inside Max cracked wide open. Something he'd been denying ever since she'd rocketed back into his life.

Swearing softly, he straightened and started toward her but she warned him off with raised hands and a quick shake of her head. "Don't. Just…don't. Let me finish this."

Hell, but he didn't want to hear the rest. He knew how this ended—with him arriving at a garden in the Hamptons too late to make a difference. He could guess the in-between. "That's why you had to go home in such a rush?"

She nodded.

"And your sister recovered?"

"Yes."

The raw note in her voice—from that cursed restraint that held her stiff and brittle and alone—cut him to the quick. He had to fist his hands around the edge of the benchtop to stop himself reaching for her. When he spoke his voice sounded almost as harsh as he felt. "So what happened? You volunteered to step into the breach?"

"I went to see David, to talk to him. The circum-stances sounded so over the top, even for my family. I thought maybe there'd been a misunderstanding. I'd always gotten along okay with David, you see, because he seemed so calm and together. I thought I could talk to him." Still battling for control of her emotions, she huffed out a shaky breath. "That's when he decided that I'd make an even better wife than Rose."

"You agreed to marry this bastard?"

"What else could I do? He had my family's finances in a death grip. My youngest sisters were still in school and he held the mortgage on both our homes. That wouldn't have mattered quite so much if the house in the Hamptons hadn't been my mother's pride and joy."

"Your father wasn't a nobody. He could have found other backing, other finance."

"He was living on past glory, on his name alone. That's why his shows had been flopping, that's why he got into trouble in the first place and grabbed David's bailout offer without thinking of the consequences."

"So you sold yourself to your father's fine upstanding business partner," he said roughly, "instead of calling me or Eliza or anyone else who could help."

"Who could help *how?*"

"By taking your father by the shirtfront and forcing him to take responsibility for his own mess. You were only twenty, for hell's sake!"

"And Rose was only eighteen and hospitalized," she countered. "Believe me, if I'd known David's true character beforehand I might not have agreed so readily. But I was young and I was gullible and I thought things would blow over with Rose, and once the financial mess was sorted I'd be able to divorce him. He promised me that out, whenever I wanted, but that was a lie. He was smart enough to keep control of my family's finances and to keep control of me."

Her words, uttered with such matter-of-fact acceptance while her eyes glimmered with those cursed tears,
knocked the stuffing right out of Max's fury. "You
should have called. You should have come to me."

"I tried to call but you weren't available. I left a note."

"A couple of cavalier lines saying you had to go
home," he said on a strangled note. "Why didn't you
find me? Why didn't you keep calling? If I'd known how
serious this was, I'd have been on the first plane to New
York." Instead of weeks later, when he'd stopped feeling
cornered by the concept of commitment, when he'd
realized that he wanted her in his life whatever it took.

"I didn't know the full story when I left Australia. All
I knew was that Rose had attempted suicide. I dashed
off a note because all I could think about was getting
home as quickly as possible. And I did call again,
several times, after I found out what was going on."

Calls he hadn't returned because he'd still been
working his way out of that corner; still pride-sore over
her abrupt departure and the offhand scribble of her
goodbye note.

"When I found out you'd taken Eva Majeur as your
date to a family wedding, I got the message."

What the…?

Shaking his head, Max laughed shortly and without
humor. "That was about as much a date as you taking
Jeffrey to Case's wedding. Eva was…convenient."

"And available," she snapped back. "She'd made that
very clear."

"Don't tell me you gave up because you thought I'd
moved on to another woman."

But that's exactly what she had thought. He could see it in her eyes. And he'd fed the idea that morning in Sky's stables, when he'd told her she was dispensable. When he'd insinuated that she had been quickly replaced.

"Does it even matter?" She dropped her shoulders and hands in a hopeless gesture. "It all happened so long ago. It doesn't serve any purpose raking over what you could have done if you'd known or if Eva hadn't been convenient or if I'd persisted. I didn't and it's history now."

"That doesn't mean I have to like it."

"I don't expect you to," she said, and her game attempt at a smile hit him in every place left open and raw by her story, by the hopelessness of frustration and regret. "I wanted to tell you the whole story," she continued, "so you know that I didn't jump from your bed into David's. I didn't choose to marry him for the sake of a wedding ring or because you'd passed on that option. I wanted you to know that."

She ended on a quiet note of finality and the ensuing silence felt heavy with weighted regrets. Max wanted to say he was sorry but he knew the apology would sound trite. As she'd pointed out a week ago, it would take a lot more than *I'm sorry* to make up for all the misunderstandings, for the pride that had stopped him calling her for too damn long, for his ugly ham-fisted accusations that day in the stables. For the insult of gifts aimed at seducing her back into his bed.

He wanted to say…hell, he didn't know what words to offer, he didn't know if anything would make a difference.

With a muffled oath he closed down the space between them and hauled her into his arms. Oh, she tried to resist but he shushed her protests and eased her head against his chest. It was all he could think to do, to offer her his support, to let her know she was no longer alone.

"It's been a rough night," he murmured, acknowledging not only the recent emotional drama but the earlier episode with her unexpected visitor. "Just let me hold you. Please."

It took about a second to recognize how right she felt in his embrace, even with her body still taut and unyielding. He stroked the length of her rigid spine until she finally started to relax. Satisfaction settled rich and sweet and belly-deep, and for a long time he just held her and stroked her back and her hair and hummed beneath his breath to the country ballad playing on her stereo.

Earlier she'd asked his preference and he'd pulled whatever CD's he recognized from her collection. They'd been playing on rotation ever since, mostly unnoticed in the background. Now the combination of the right music and the right woman in his arms eased the deep ache in his chest a notch. The past could not be undone; he couldn't fix what had happened then, no matter how badly he wished it otherwise.

"There's one more thing I have to ask." Tension strummed the edges of his mood but he soothed it by coiling a tress of her cool, silky hair around his fingers. "Did he ever hurt you?"

She eased back a fraction.

"Your husband…was he abusive?"

"He wasn't violent," she said softly, "if that's what you're asking."

It was something, he supposed, a very small solace when he sensed she'd been wounded in many other ways.

"Can we move on now?" she asked. "I've had enough of the past for one night."

"If that's what you want."

She rested her cheek against his chest and her hands, finally, stretched from their loose hold on his waist to caress his back. He wasn't sure of her exact words, muffled against his shirt, but he thought she said, "That's what I want."

For a long time that was enough. Diana in his arms. The scent of her hair warm and familiar.

"You still use the same shampoo." He tucked a loose strand of hair behind her ear, touched a finger to the tiny pearl stud in her ear. "Are these the same earrings?"

She nodded, a delicious stroke of friction over his heart. "You remember."

"I remember."

For one whole weekend she'd worn little more than those earrings. He'd felt them beneath his tongue, a cool hard contrast to the warm responsive skin that he'd loved so well, so thoroughly, so often.

The memory surged through his blood and made a mockery of his murmured request to just hold her. He supposed the only surprise here was that their own special brand of electricity had taken half a CD to spark to life. Where Diana was concerned, a couple of bars of the opening track and her body swaying against his should have flicked the switch to full power.

And her body *was* swaying against his, he suddenly noticed, although so infinitesimally she may not even have realized she was responding to the melody playing around them. He smiled and looped his arms around her back. "I was going to take you dancing tonight."

"Whereabouts?"

"The Badlands Bar."

She laughed, a sultry puff of sound that warmed through his shirt to the overheated skin beneath.

"We could still go if you want." But he tucked her closer into his body and swayed in time to the soaring final chorus. "Although this is rather nice."

Nice lasted to the end of the song before she went still. One of her hands clenched in his shirt for the beat of silence before the next track started and for that single second he felt the shift of her hips and the subtle pressure of her belly against his erection.

There was nothing subtle about his male reaction.

The primal hum of desire thickened in his blood and with a low groan he slid his hands lower to cup her backside, to press her closer. She lifted her head and he saw a note of hesitancy in her eyes, a shadow of vulnerability that wakened a possessive tenderness stronger than he'd ever felt before.

This was his woman and he wasn't letting go.

Slowly he eased his grip and gentled his touch, lifting his hands in a long, slow caress from hips to waist to shoulders. Then he brushed the backs of his fingers against her cheek, stroked his thumb over her bottom lip. And when he bent his head to kiss her, when he tasted the familiar warmth of her lips, he tempered the surge of male need and moved his mouth over hers with restrained patience.

It was a kiss of comfort, an extension of the *I-just-want-to-hold-you* hug, and when he sensed the same hesitancy in her response as he'd read in her expression a moment before, he felt a powerful urge to plunder, to take the decision from her hands, to sway her with the force of their chemistry.

Yet he knew that wasn't the way. Not after what he'd learned about the coercion that had led to her marriage.

Their next kiss would be at her inception, their next embrace at her command, and when she became his lover again, it would be her choice. Her seduction.

Reluctantly he broke away from the kiss and watched as she blinked his mouth and then his face into focus. One of her hands had strayed to his neck and her fingertips trailed like butterfly wings against the ends of his hair as she retreated. She would touch him again, he promised himself, in that same provocative way.

Except the next time they would both be naked.

Because he couldn't let her go completely, he cupped her upper arms in his hands and waited for her gaze to fasten on his.

"So, the dance is over." Underneath the flushed skin of her throat, her pulse beat with those same butterfly wings. "What now?"

"That's up to you," he told her. "I'm staying here tonight, in case your intruder returns. Whether I sleep in your bed or the guestroom is your call."

"No pressure, huh?"

"I've never pressured you into sleeping with me, Diana."

"There are different kinds of pressure."

Max's gaze narrowed as he figured out her meaning. "I'm not apologizing for the fact you turn me on. Just because a gun's loaded doesn't mean a man is going to use it."

"Are you saying you're going to walk away, without trying anything?"

"I'll walk right to your guestroom if that's what you choose."

He'd surprised her but it gave him little satisfaction because the suspicion was back in her eyes. Right when he had no agenda, right when he was doing the noble and gentlemanly thing. That mistrust chafed at his patience. So did the stretch of hesitation without an answer.

"Either you want to sleep with me," he said, "or you don't. It's as simple as that. This isn't a trick question, there's no hidden agenda. I thought you might appreciate making the decision without me pushing you."

She stared up at him a moment, still wary-eyed, and then she laughed. She straight-out, fair dinkum laughed. Then she shook her head. "I'm sorry, but I'm sure force is hardwired into your genes. You are chronically unable to *not* push."

"What is that supposed to mean?"

"It means that you still have your hands on me, reminding me how much better those hands feel on my bare skin. It means you gave me exactly three seconds to make up my mind before you implied I was taking too long over a simple question and pushed me—yes, you did push me, Max!—for an answer." She paused to draw breath. "Except it isn't as simple as yes or no for me. I know it should be, but it isn't."

"So your answer is no?"

"If you need it right this second, then I guess it is."

He nodded curtly. "Then you'd better point me in the direction of your guestroom."

Diana hated watching him walk away.

As soon as he'd left her, alone and chilled by his rapid departure, she kicked herself for handling the situation so badly. It had been a knee-jerk reaction, the laughter, her sardonic tone, even if her words were the simple and honest truth.

Max *always* had an agenda, a purpose, a goal which he pursued with a relentless aim of success. The fact that he had backed off, that he hadn't pushed his advantage when she'd been at her most vulnerable, was something she should have thanked him for, not insulted him over. He'd loaned her his strength when she'd been close to falling apart, he'd distracted her shattered emotions by joking over dancing at the local honky-tonk, he'd kissed her with disciplined tenderness. He'd stayed the night to protect her.

And he'd handed her exactly what she needed: the opportunity to go to him on her own terms, strong in the knowledge that she'd made the choice without any persuasion.

All through the night she debated taking the short walk to the adjoining bedroom, to apologize, to explain. But there was only one reason to go to him and she knew this was not the right time. Still raw from the scare of

Gregg's intrusion, still hollow from all she'd spilled in her painful revelations about her marriage, she was too susceptible and needy. Too open to the suggestion that this could be more than a night of sex with the ex.

Eventually she slept the sleep of the emotionally drained. In the morning she would apologize. In the morning she would decide.

Diana woke early, as was her habit, but Max had woken earlier. Padding to the kitchen to start coffee, she found him in her sunroom and stopped short. A mug in one hand, the other propped against the window frame, he stood gazing out the window at her snow-covered yard.

He wasn't wearing a shirt.

She couldn't look away.

But it wasn't the stretch of bare skin across his shoulders and down to the waist of low-riding dark trousers that ambushed her attention. It wasn't the strong curve of his biceps or the softer, paler line of his underarm. It was the way the morning sunlight slanted across his face, highlighting the plane between cheekbone and jaw and silvering the ends of his bed-tousled hair.

Her fingers itched for her camera. To capture the warm hews of his skin and the blunt strength of his bone structure against the softened mounds of powdery snow…

He shifted suddenly, straightening from his leaning posture, and Diana backed up a few quick steps. She felt oddly shy in her nightwear. And nervous of what she had to say, of how she might word her request.

But he hadn't sensed her presence. He seemed distracted and she saw tension in the tightly bunched muscles across his shoulders. The fingers of his free hand curled into a fist and he punched the window frame, not solidly, but with a contained frustration that grabbed her by the throat.

Then he turned and saw her and for several seconds she couldn't think or speak or move.

"I made coffee," he said, and his voice still held an edge of morning gruffness. "I hope you don't mind."

"Of course not. I'm glad you found everything. Did you sleep well?"

A silly question, she realized, as soon as his forest-dark gaze stilled on her face. "Did you?"

"Not so well," she admitted.

Now was her chance to apologize for last night, but before she could compose the necessary words he spoke, his tone brusque, his message pointed. "You need to go to the police about your trespasser. And this place is begging for a decent security system. He proved last night he could walk right up to your front door, and look at this." He swept an arm toward the window. "From the park out the back, you can see right through here."

Diana's gaze swept over the view he indicated with a new consciousness. Goose bumps broke out along her skin, and they owed less to the winter landscape than to the fear attached to his blunt comments. She wrapped the warm robe more firmly around her middle but that didn't halt the chill beneath her skin. "If it makes you feel any better, I will talk to the police."

"When?"

"Look, I'm not going to let Gregg into the house if

he returns. And you're scaring me with this talk about security and people looking into my home."

"Good, if that's what it takes. Because when I was walking up your path last night…when I heard that breaking china and raised voices…"

His voice stopped abruptly, but his harrowed expression took over where the words left off. Never would he admit it, but he'd been genuinely frightened for her safety. Diana's vexation with his bossiness dissolved into mush.

Her expression softened. "You really do care."

"Yeah, I care. I hate the thought of walking out of here, not knowing you'll be safe."

His tone was rough with an emotion that made Diana's heart skip several beats. It restarted somewhere higher in her chest and she knew this was it. Her decision made in the space of a heartbeat and in the end it wasn't even difficult. "You would know I was safe if I came with you."

"To Kentucky?"

"Yes." Her gaze met his with steady certainty and they both knew what she was saying yes to. "I would love to come with you, if your invitation still holds."

Eight

They traveled in the Fortune's private jet, arriving at Lexington's Bluegrass Field shortly after ten. The manager of the stallion syndicate sent a car to meet them. When the driver, who introduced himself as Roland K. Abraham, learned that Diana had never visited their county before, he took it upon himself to transport them to their hotel via the scenic route.

"Only if that doesn't hold up your meeting." Diana turned worried eyes to Max. "What time do you need to be at the hotel?"

"We got plenty of time," the driver assured her via the rearview mirror. "The boss won' be arriving at the hotel for more than an hour yet."

"Do you want to see the sights?" Max asked.

"'Course she does," Roland interceded. "Everybody

needs to see why Bluegrass County makes the world's fastest horses and the world's smoothest bourbon."

He didn't allow them an opening to refute those claims before launching into an eloquent monologue that hit all the high points of his home for the past sixty-three years. "Born here and never felt inclined to leave," he divulged, before pausing to point out the Keeneland Racecourse.

"Best park in the country." At length he told them why, a blur of names and facts that meant nothing to Diana. "You ever been racing here?" he asked Max.

"I haven't had that pleasure."

"You need to rectify that real quick. Bring your wife back in the springtime. Buy her a pretty hat, take her racing on Stakes day." He whistled softly through his teeth. "Yessirree, all those pretty fillies make that a fine day's racing."

Diana snuck a peek at Max's face. He didn't look perturbed by the driver's casual assumption that they were a married couple. And she could hardly correct the man.

Um, sorry to disillusion you, Roland, but I'm just along for the ride.

Warmth bloomed beneath her skin when she recognized her unintentional double-entendre. On top of Roland's reference to women as fillies, that flip comment would definitely have left the wrong impression. Just as well she had kept silent.

Except the meaning behind the unspoken words—the meaning behind her presence here at Max's side—reawakened and rippled through her senses...as it had done a score of times since making her decision early that morning. She wanted to take a leaf from Max's apparent impassivity. He'd said little all morning. If anything he seemed slightly distant, distracted no doubt by the upcoming round of meetings.

She understood, but that didn't help calm her growing anxiety. In her mind she wanted to be Strong Sexual Woman, able to have this man she desired, to take pleasure from his body and to want nothing more. But in her heart she doubted she owned that ability.

Despite genetics, she'd never been the best at role play. She'd failed miserably in the acting classes she'd been forced to take. She'd hated every minute of every class.

"Diana?"

Zoning back in, she found both pairs of male eyes watching her. Waiting for an answer…? She pulled an apologetic face. "Sorry, I was woolgathering."

"Roland asked if the heating was too high. Would you like it turned down?"

"Yes. Thank you. It is warm," she lied, pretty sure the question had been prompted by a flushed face that owed nothing to the temperature.

"How long you folks fixin' on staying?"

"That depends," Max said evenly, "on how things work out."

Diana's tummy jumped into her throat. Business, she reminded herself. He's talking about business.

"If you stay on for the weekend, you'll be needin' your heating. They're predicting some wild weather."

"Snow?" Max asked.

"So they say. As you can see—" he angled his head

to indicate the rolling fields outside "—we already had a few inches this week."

The fields were coated in a layer of white so smooth it might have been painted on. Everything, she noted, was neat and manicured. Mile after mile of wooden fences, the lines of posts meticulously straight. Avenues of trees standing in soldierly ranks. Stud farm entrances signposted in gilded lettering beside ornate iron gates.

It was all so unlike the scrambling disorder of her nerves.

The men were still discussing the weather—snowstorms here were worthy of discussion, apparently—and then how black fences were replacing white in some places. They were cheaper to maintain, according to their expert guide. Diana listened selectively until the conversation moved on to a particular farm they were passing and she realized that Max knew rather a lot about it.

"You've visited here?" Diana asked.

"This is where I bought the mare."

"Maggie?" Neck craned to study the farm's impressive entranceway, she didn't realize her unconscious use of the nickname until she felt his questioning gaze on her face.

"Maggie?" he repeated. "Are we talking about the same horse?"

So she told him about the day of the photography shoot and how she'd come up with the name.

"You renamed my horse?"

"I *nick*named your horse. It's a technique I use. A bonding between me and my subject," she said haughtily, self-conscious that she might sound daft and very aware that his attention was fully on her for the first time since they'd left Sioux Falls. "You don't have to like my choice of name. You can stick with Bootylicious," she added.

She'd thought he might laugh or at least joke about that name, but she was wrong.

"I like it," he said in a low voice, and his appreciative gaze caused a ripple of pleasure to roll through her body. "And here I was thinking you didn't like horses."

"Maggie might be the exception."

"You have excellent taste," he said.

"I know."

He smiled at that, but then he seemed to become lost in her eyes and she wondered if he could read the message so boldly emblazoned on her brain.

I do have excellent taste, I chose you as my lover. My only lover.

"Glad you came?" he asked.

"We'll see."

The smile faded from his eyes, leaving them dark and serious and intense. "Just remember, it's your choice. No pressure."

Diana discovered that she hadn't believed him, not in her heart, until they checked in at the hotel.

There'd been an awkward moment as they walked across the lobby of the elegant old-English-style lodging and a booming Midwestern voice hailed Max. The syndicate manager, Roy Crowley, strode up to them with two colleagues in tow. While the men shook hands, Diana tensed, waiting to see how he handled her introduction.

"This is a friend of mine, Diana Fielding," he said.

No uncomfortable pause while he considered how to qualify her status and for that she forgave his use of her maiden name. She smiled, relaxing, because he'd made it so easy.

Or he would have done, if one of the men hadn't missed her name.

"Diana Young," she told him as they shook hands, unaware of the unconscious contradiction until she felt all eyes on her.

"Wasn't it Fielding?" Crowley asked.

"It was," Max said shortly. "But now it's Young."

Needless to say, all the men looked confused and when Max excused himself so they could check in, Crowley said, "No need. Your room's taken care off. It's a junior suite, has its own sitting room. Very spacious." His gaze shifted to Diana. "I hope you're comfortable there, ma'am."

Which is when Max smoothly interceded to say they required separate rooms. In that moment Diana realized that anything from here on in really *would* be her choice, instigated by her first move. "Thank you," she said quietly as they crossed to the front desk.

"You're welcome."

Crowley invited her to join the group for lunch, insisting they wouldn't bore her with horse talk. He was wrong...and he was right. They did talk horses right through the long meal but she was far from bored.

Seeing Max in his element was a revelation. He didn't dominate the conversation as Crowley and a younger wise-mouth lawyer attempted to do, yet when he did speak he commanded the whole table's attention. He didn't have to condescend or try to make an impression. He did that through his knowledge and sharp observations. Diana was captivated.

At one point, when he countered a loud assertion by the lawyer with quick logic, she'd wanted to stand and applaud. But then she realized this wasn't a performance. This was simply Max, doing what he did best, and making her fall even more deeply under his spell.

That sobering thought sat her back in her chair for the remainder of the meal.

Later, when the men moved to a meeting room to get down to business, she grabbed her camera and took a walk. After spending several hours in her element, doing what she did best, fading light sent her back to her hotel room. But she felt good, invigorated, happy, and the prospect of the night ahead—of, for the first time in her life, being the seducer instead of the seducee—only caused her heart to beat faster with anticipation rather than with the nerves that had assailed her during their morning travel.

Washing her hair reminded her of the previous night in her kitchen, when Max had stroked the loose tresses and commented on the familiar scent. She applied extra conditioner, rich with the warm notes of vanilla and amber. The whipped body soufflé she worked into her skin, all over, had notes of the same fragrance.

She was almost done primping when Max called to see if she would like to join them for dinner.

"Have you wrapped up business?" she asked, sounding all sensible and calm despite the thump-thump-thump of her elevated heartbeat.

"Not quite. Pettit is being obstructive."

The know-it-all lawyer. "That figures."

"Looks like we'll be thrashing this out for a while yet."

"Then I'll pass on joining you for dinner," she decided. "Let you continue your thrashing without inhibition."

He tried to change her mind but she insisted she would be happier ordering room service. When he started to object to that, she silenced him by saying, "Look, I'm just out of the shower and, really, I'd as soon not have to get dressed."

After a beat of silence he recovered. "You might want to get dressed before you open the door to room service."

Smiling, she coiled the phone cord around her hand. "Will you let me know how your meeting ends up?"

"It might be late," he warned.

"I don't mind. I'd really like to know. I'll put some champagne on ice in case you want to celebrate."

Diana came awake slowly. Foggy with disorientation it took a moment to place herself. Lexington. The King George Hotel. Sitting room in the suite. Someone knocking on the door....

She sat up in a rush. Max. She'd nodded off while waiting for his very late meeting to finish. She'd insisted he let her know the result.

Instantly alert, she wrapped the sash of her robe more snugly around her middle and padded to the door. She swung it open in a rush and found Max glowered down at her. "Didn't you learn your lesson last night about opening the door to anyone who knocks?"

She was too pleased to see him, even tired and scowling, to take exception. "Not anyone," she told him, opening the door wider. "Only you."

Max had been about to ask how the hell she knew it was him, but the way she said "only you" and the way she stepped back from the door to usher him inside, wiped the reprimand from his tongue and the weariness from both mind and body.

He accepted the unspoken invitation and followed the sway of her white-robed hips into the cozy sitting room. A log fire flickered in one corner. Classic R & B crooned from the stereo speakers. She turned the volume down a notch.

"I'm sorry I didn't hear you. I must have dozed off. Would you like a drink?"

"Please."

She pulled the promised bottle of champagne from a standing ice bucket and arched a brow. "Are we toasting a successful deal?"

"We are but I need something stronger than champagne." He poured himself a liberal glass from a bottle of bourbon on the bar.

"Success?" she asked. "Signed, sealed, delivered?"

"Not quite delivered, but yeah. We've shaken hands."

And her wide smile made up for all the day's aggravations, for all of Pettit's posturing and Crowley's blustery speeches. Abandoning the French sparkly, she poured her own glass of the hard stuff—only half-full he noticed—and clinked it against his. "Cheers."

Their eyes met above the rims of their lifted glasses. The local blend packed quite a kick but not as much as the warmth in her eyes.

"You look tired," she said. "Sit."

He wasn't tired any more but he sat, mostly because she'd curled herself into one corner of the plushly upholstered lounge. He took the other end and watched as she tucked one leg up under her bottom. Her bare foot arched over the edge of the seat and he wondered if she wore anything beneath the plush white robe. He hoped she wouldn't keep him wondering long.

"Do you want to talk?" she asked. "Or would you rather just unwind."

"I'm all done with talking business. Why don't you tell me how you spent your afternoon?"

She told him about her long walk through the streets of Lexington, about the places she'd seen and the photos she'd taken, and he found himself unwinding much more than he could have imagined when she'd opened that door. When he'd wondered what kind of disappointment he was setting himself up for by coming knocking so late at night, especially after she'd taken so long to answer. He sipped his drink and he listened to the enthusiasm in her voice and watched the muted passion in her eyes as she explained the whyfors and whathaveyous of her shots.

Then she stopped, her expression suddenly self-conscious, a flush of pink rising from inside her robe to color her throat. "I'm sorry. I'm putting you to sleep."

"Never."

She must have realized then that his gaze had dipped

from her throat to the deep V of her crossover robe. To the shadowed curve of one breast. She didn't rush to cover up. She took a slow sip from her glass and allowed him his second's peep show.

Then, when his gaze lifted to meet hers, she said, "It's been a long day. You look done in."

"I'm ready for bed."

Another slow second passed, while banked heat and steady resolve and something else darkened her eyes. While the crooner on the stereo sang, *here I am, baby*. She reached across and took the glass from his hand. "So am I," she said. "Would you like to take a shower first?"

Oh, yeah. He most definitely would.

Diana thought about joining him in the shower, but vanity prevailed. She'd spent the better part of an hour blow-drying her thick hair and creaming her skin and applying the subtlest of makeup. She waited for him in bed, naked but surprisingly calm. When she felt the sensuous slide of her skin against the cool sheets, she decided that in future she would always sleep nude. And only between superfine Egyptian cotton sheets.

The thought amused her and she was still smiling at herself—or at the superconfident woman who'd invaded her body—when the shower stopped. Everything inside her seemed to pause, as well, like an indrawn breath of anticipation. She closed her eyes and counted to ten, then to twenty, and slowly on to thirty, and her inner tension sharpened to a point akin to pain. She'd left the stereo on, the low volume enough to mask the sound of bare feet on carpet.

Yet she knew he was there.

Opening her eyes, she came up on both elbows and found him in the doorway, wearing one of the hotel robes and holding his refilled glass in one hand. Twin bedside lamps cast a warm glow over the king-size bed but he stood in shadow, his face all square strength and shadowed planes, his jaw dark with evening stubble, his hair wet and towel mussed. The image was slightly un-civilized, far removed from the urbane businessman at lunch, a world apart from the easygoing cowboy she'd fallen so hard for ten years before.

But her body remembered his touch and the mem-ories hummed in her blood and quieted the race of her heartbeat to a deep rhythm. Her gaze remained steady on his and when she spoke her voice sounded calm and composed. "Are you coming to bed?"

"When I finish my drink."

"Bring it with you," she said. "I've developed a liking for it."

He didn't move, except to lift the glass infinitesi-mally. "How much have you had, exactly?"

Slowly she rose to a sitting position, the crisp white sheet tucked loosely beneath her arms. "I beg your pardon?"

"I want to be sure that you know what you're doing."

"I know what I'm doing, Max. You gave me plenty of time to reconsider and I didn't need more than one nip of bourbon for courage. But if you'd like me to pass a sobriety test, I'll walk the straight line over to you."

A smile tugged at the corners of his mouth—possibly at her primly offended tone—and for a second she thought he would take her up on the offer. Which would serve her right for being a smarty pants. But then he straightened off the doorjamb and started toward her, circling the big bed with unhurried strides. "Tempting," he said softly, "but I rather like you where you are."

"You didn't used to mind where."

Their eyes met and the air sparked with super-charged memories of those *wheres* and with burning anticipation of the *hows*. Mesmerized, Diana didn't notice that he'd looped a clever finger in the sheet until he tugged it down. Until he leaned closer and she held her breath anticipating his kiss, only to lose that breath in a swift hiss when a tiny spill from his glass trickled down the skin he'd stripped bare.

A deliberate spill, she realized, when he leaned forward to lick it from her skin. He took his sweet time tracking from the hollow at her throat to the dip of her belly-button, and the lazy stroke of his tongue reso-nated in every female cell she possessed.

When he was done he came up to meet her eyes. "I seem to be developing a liking for it, too."

Stunned by his audacity and by the intensity of the reaction that rippled through her body, Diana took several seconds to work out the connection. She'd told him to bring his glass with him because she'd developed a liking for the local bourbon. And this is how the clever devil responded.

"Are you going to share?" she asked.

"My drink? Or are you referring to something else?"

She smiled and stroked the bed at her side. "Why don't you sit down here and we'll negotiate."

"I've had more than enough negotiating for one day. Let's assume I'm up for sharing." He lifted his hands in a have-at-me gesture. "I'm all yours."

A giddying thought. One Diana didn't give herself a chance to mull over for fear she'd lose her grip on the teasing mood. Instead she dipped her hand through the sash on his robe and used the leverage to tug him down onto the bed. She lifted both hands to cradle his face and ran her thumbs across the fullness of his bottom lip, such a smooth contrast to the whiskery rasp of his jaw.

"Cool hands," he murmured. Turning his face within their gentle hold, he pressed his mouth against the palm of one hand and then the other and the warm sensation exploded through her veins to fill her chest.

"Warm mouth," she murmured, leaning in to kiss him with the same sensual tenderness. She pulled back an inch, enough to look into his eyes before she whispered. "Thank you."

There was a beat of silence before he asked, "For?"

"For understanding that I needed to make this decision."

"No need to thank me. I'm right where I always wanted to be."

A sliver of unease prodded at the back of her mind but she shut it out. He was teasing. And she followed suit, spreading one of her hands wide in the center of his chest and pushing him down against the mattress. "You're on your back. That is not your favorite position."

"Says who?" A hand on the back of her head eased her closer to his mouth. "This is one of my very favorite positions."

He closed the whisper of space to kiss her, at first in

gentle exploration and then with increasing ardor, a giving open-mouthed kiss that tasted of bourbon and longing, a delicious combination of the new and the familiar.

Then his tongue slid against hers and the desire surged through her body, instant and achingly intense. The hand cupping the back of her head shifted, changing the angle of the kiss and of her body. Her breasts brushed against his chest, sharpening the ache into acute points of need.

So very quickly the kiss wasn't enough.

For an instant she entertained the notion of chasing a bourbon spill down his body as he had done with her, but no. She was hungry for the taste of his skin on her tongue, clean and untainted. For the feel of his hard muscled body tensing beneath her hands. For that moment of heart-stopping connection when she took him inside her body.

I'm all yours, he'd said, and she claimed him with her mouth, kissing him from collar bone to collar bone then working her way down the hard stretch of his abdomen, opening his robe and pushing it aside as she went. When she lay her open mouth against his exposed belly, when she rolled a long full-tongued lick across his skin, he sucked in an audible breath.

"Below the belt," he murmured.

"Technically, I'm still above the belt."

She hadn't forgotten his size. She hadn't forgotten the alluring combination of velvet and steel, or the intoxicating power she wielded with the stroke of a finger and the touch of her tongue. Nor had she forgotten the crown-shaped birthmark, so perfectly formed it might have been tattooed into the lean dip of his flank. She traced it with the tip of her index finger and then with her lips, and when he groaned for mercy she kissed her way back up to his mouth.

For a long while she immersed herself in the delicious subtleties of that kiss, giving back all that she could remember and more than she'd forgotten. They sank into the softness of the bed, rolling in a sensuous twining of limbs and sheets and sighs. She barely noticed when he came out of the kiss on top. She didn't mind that he'd taken control; she didn't care because his big skilful hands were gliding down her body, rediscovering her breasts and her belly, the dip of her back and the inner stretch of her thighs with a deliciously unhurried thoroughness.

He kissed her throat, bit the sensitive slope of her shoulder, sucked the tight ache of each nipple, and every sensation built upon the last in a spiraling sensual assault that stole her breath. Hands clutched in the sheets, she rolled her head back on the piled feathery pillows and arched her back in silent invitation. He obliged, sliding down her belly, the hot torment of his mouth everywhere at once, too much but never enough, driving her to the brink of climax then leaving her adrift and trembling.

Then he kissed her again, with her taste on his lips and his need dark and fervent in his eyes. Skin to skin, they stilled, his big body hot and heavy between her thighs. Slowly he stretched her arms above her head, fingers twining in a bond that felt as intimate as the connection of their bodies. A shiver rippled through her, tense and anticipatory.

"Now this," he murmured, "is my very favorite position. I'm right where I always wanted to be."

And I'm all yours, her soul whispered back, as wide open and welcoming as her body that took him inside. Their gazes melded to complete the connection, deep, total, complete, and the swell of emotion in her chest drove all the breath from her lungs.

In that instant she knew that she'd lied to him and to herself. She had no clue what she was doing here, and no capacity to separate her emotions from the physical or from the sensual. She couldn't take him so completely into her body without taking him into her heart.

It was much too late to do anything about it and, worse, when he started to move in her she didn't even care.

Tilting her hips, she wrapped her legs higher on his sweat-dampened back and drew him deeper, urging him to build the intensity, seeking the perfect angle and the perfect bliss that shimmered on the rim of her senses. Drawing the delicious heat into her heart.

Arms stretched higher, their fingers caught and gripped, their gazes fired by the explosive heat of their connection.

"This is the together I remember."

"I remember," she replied on a low exhalation. "Our chemistry is an awfully powerful thing."

Something dark sparked deep in his eyes, a retraction, an objection, or perhaps an acknowledgement of that conversation, when she'd been so busily protecting herself and her feelings.

"Awful is the wrong word," he said tightly, paused above her, holding them both on the edge. "This is never awful."

That was all he said before driving them both to a release that was powerful and prolonged, wild and wonderful.

Later they lay face to face, cooling breaths mingling and binding them together, while her heart ached in lonely certainty that *this* was all he would ever want from her. Sex—wonderful, wild, always powerful, always fulfilling. She went to sleep wishing that it could be enough.

Nine

They made love again in the dark of early morning and again with dawn sunbeams dancing across the bed, and yet it still wasn't enough to fill the hollow depths of Max's hunger. He asked her to stay another day and she agreed without pause. As a reward he let her have her way with him. Not that it was any hardship letting her honeyed tongue work its magic, feeling the cool sweep of her hair over his skin, seeing the utter abandonment on her face when she rode him to her climax. Later he gave it all back, every touch, every taste, every long drawn-out sigh of pleasure. It may have been ten years, she might claim to be a different person, but he still knew every way to make her beg for mercy…and then for more.

What he didn't know was how to tell her of the fullness in his chest or the rightness in his heart whenever he sank deep into her heat. What he didn't know was how to bind her to him, to make their together last. He didn't have the words or the answers. All he could do was show her.

Diana felt bound to mention the predicted rough weather but he shrugged it off with "I'm not planning on leaving this suite." Cocooned in that safe haven, they didn't much care when widespread whiteouts shut down airports across a half-dozen states, although the ensuing chaos left them stranded for a second and then a third day. Hearing the news, Max pulled her back under the covers and promised to keep her warm.

Ever diligent and always the perfectionist, he set about keeping that promise…and not only in the bedroom.

Diana discovered how easily he could warm her from the inside out through simple shared pleasures. Games of backgammon where she, the expert, kicked his butt and his ego all around the suite and back again. Smiling over his determination to complete a gigantic old-fashioned jigsaw puzzle…of a snowstorm. Laughing as he chased her down to confiscate her camera after she'd snapped a series of candid shots of him buff and beautiful. He was very diligent in supervising their deletion.

They talked, too, skimming the edges of the years they'd been apart. Max told her about the expansion of his family's cattle ranching business and sketched out the many other businesses in which he held a stake. Many were in partnership with his friend Zack. He told her how a day out at the Melbourne Cup had fuelled his and Zack's plan to start the racehorse stud.

"Is the Melbourne Cup a horse race?" she asked.

"It's Australia's biggest horse race," he told her, "and one of our biggest days out. You know how Roland talked about the Bluegrass Stakes with the well-dressed fillies out on parade? Well, that's a similar picture to our Cup day. People dress up to the nines, they hold all-day picnics in the car park and in marquees on the racecourse lawns."

"So you and Zack hatched a plan to lure all the well-dressed fillies into your marquee?" she teased.

"I prefer them undressed." In bed at the time, he stroked a hand down her undressed flank but the seriousness in his eyes belied the teasing mood. "We decided to breed a Melbourne Cup winner."

Not they *wanted* to, they *decided* to. "Surely that isn't something you can just do. There has to be a lot of luck involved."

"Study, smart investment, commitment, drive. They all combine to make luck."

Diana didn't disagree. She supposed she'd made her own luck with her photography, using some of those very skills. She stroked a hand over his chest, over the steady beat of his heart, and she remembered another time in another bed. Another conversation about dreams, more than a decade old.

"Did you ever build your yacht?" she asked.

He didn't answer right away and there was an unsettling quality to his silence that made Diana wonder if he remembered….

"You told me once, that a yacht was your ultimate purchase," she explained. "A big fancy cruiser you could moor on Sydney harbor."

Because of his outback upbringing, Max had had a fascination with water, with the smooth speed and graceful power of the big boats on the harbor. "Dreams change," he said shortly. "I moved on."

That particular dream had moved on with her, shoved aside along with the diamond solitaire and the dreams of carrying her over the threshold into the stateroom before they set sail on their honeymoon. He hadn't allowed himself to think about that dream in years. He didn't want to discuss it now. Smoothly he steered the conversation on, relating a long anecdote that involved his brother Brody's boating misadventure in the Whitsunday Passage. Somehow that led to him telling her stuff he'd never intended about his family, his nieces and nephews, the three he was godfather to.

"The eternal lot of the single brother," he quipped.

She smiled but her hand on his chest stilled with the same tension he felt in her willowy body. "So, you didn't ever marry?"

"Almost did once," he answered, with a tight hitch of his shoulder. "Never been tempted since."

"Lucky you," she murmured after a moment.

The emotion triggered by those two telling words punched him hard in the solar plexus. With one phone call this all could have played out so differently for them both.

Yeah, he thought bitterly. *I'm one lucky son of a gun.*

When they couldn't fly out until Monday afternoon, Diana recalled her real world obligations long enough to call in absent from work. Jeffrey didn't answer at home, the gallery or his cell phone. After trying numerous times over many hours, she wondered if the storms had closed Sioux Falls down. She couldn't think of any other reason for the *Click* phone to go unanswered for so long.

Slightly concerned she called Eliza to pass on the message.

Eliza chuckled. "I don't think your absence will be noticed, somehow. The city is working overtime to clear the roads and I can't imagine many businesses opening today. No one in their right mind would venture out of doors for anything but necessities!"

Relieved, Diana made to end the call but Eliza was too quick. "Where, exactly, are you snowed in? I don't suppose it's somewhere in Kentucky? Maybe near... hmm...let me think...Lexington? Am I warm?"

"You are. Very."

"I knew it! Although I bet I'm not nearly as warm as you two!"

Blushing, Diana glanced across the room to where Max seemed engrossed in flicking between sports channels. But Max was a skilled multi-tasker. For example, he was amazingly adept with hands and mouth and a certain other body part, all at the one time. In comparison, listening to three alternate channels and one phone conversation would be child's play!

"I can't exactly talk right now," she murmured into the phone.

"Okay, so I'll just ask a couple of quick yes-or-no questions and leave you to your fun. Things *are* fun, right?"

"Right." Although her heart did a serious lurch just from watching Max stretch his shoulders and neck—without even needing to hark back to their earlier exchange about family. The look on his face when he'd talked about his youngest goddaughter, Alice, and the puppy he'd given her for Christmas. The telling lack of expression when he told her how he'd almost married once. The yearning in her heart had created an over-whelming, almost crippling pain.

No. That had not been fun.

"And you have talked?" Eliza asked. "You told him why you had to marry? You cleared up that misunderstanding?"

"Yes."

"I'm so glad. Secrets are not good for the soul. They eat away at your peace of mind long after they have any right to."

Diana recalled detecting a similar tone in her friend's voice the last time they'd lunched, something that hinted at a deeper meaning behind the idle advice. Yet Eliza harboring secrets? She'd never known her friend to be anything but frank and open. It seemed so unlikely, and yet...

"Is there something bothering you, Eliza? Some deep, dark secret you're longing to get off your chest?"

"Oh, we all have secrets," Eliza replied blithely, before ending the conversation with the direction to, "Enjoy what's left of your weekend."

Enjoying the weekend hadn't been difficult, not while she concentrated on the now and studiously ignored the what-comes-next. But after they left the hotel on Monday afternoon and commenced the trip back to Sioux Falls, that question loomed larger and larger with each passing mile. They had left Fantasyland behind. Soon they would return to the real world, the real world where he would return to Australia and she would not.

The notion of saying goodbye had tied Diana in a twisted pretzel of anxiety by the time they arrived at her home. Max had been silent on the drive, wrapped in thoughts that set his jaw tight. She dared not ask. A full schedule of acting and speech and etiquette classes had packed her childhood, and a fat lot of good they were proving now. She did not know what to say. Thank you and goodbye seemed vastly inadequate.

As they turned into her street and approached her home, Diana peeked a quick sideways glance at her silent companion, at the grim, hard lines of his face and the tick of a muscle in his cheek. The tendrils of apprehension that had twisted through her system banded steely tight in her chest. This was not going to be easy. Added to the farewell, she knew memories of his last visit to her home and his fear over her intruder would be riding him hard.

She searched for a distracting comment, something to bridge the awful tension, but before she could utter a word Max's posture stiffened. His big hands tightened on the wheel. "That car." He nodded to indicate the white sedan blocking the entrance to her garage. "Is there any reason it should be in your drive?"

"I don't know," she replied slowly. "Unless it's Gregg."

"That's what I thought."

"Except…I haven't been home. Why would he still be hanging around?"

Max didn't care about the *whys*. He didn't intend asking for any when he found the creep, either. He stopped the car in the street and turned to Diana. "Give me your keys."

"Do you think he's in the house?"

"That's what I'm going to find out," Max said tightly. The thought that he might have broken in, that he might have done so at another time and found Diana here alone, afraid, defenseless, near choked him with fury. "Stay here. I won't be long."

This time he didn't bother checking the car. He went straight to the house, eyes scanning the snow-covered front garden for any signs of movement in the long shadows of late afternoon. No footprints in the snow, no broken windows in the front of the house, no signs of forced entry.

Inside the house lay silent and visibly untouched. Quickly he moved from room to room, finding nothing but a keen edge of disappointment. A primal part of him had wanted to find the creep, had wanted an excuse to make him regret coming back here. But he suppressed it because of the distress on Diana's face when she'd considered that he might be in her home. Because of the tremor in her cold hands as she handed over the keys.

Because he wanted to protect her from all those fears, to shield her from all distress, to drive every thought and every memory and every impact of David Young from her consciousness.

After one run through the house, Max knew the

stepson wasn't inside. So where the hell was he? Certain he would find him lurking somewhere, inside or out, he'd ordered Diana to stay in the car. Now he experienced a wrench of misgiving. He'd been gone a couple of minutes, five at the most, yet suddenly that felt like four-and-a-half too many.

He hurried to the front door and out through the courtyard, breath backing up in his lungs until he could see the car again.

She wasn't in it.

"Diana."

Heart pounding, he yelled her name and the gasp of her choked reply—not quite his name, not even a whole word—sliced through the silence and into his blood like a cold knife of fear. A sign of movement beyond the rental car, in the shadows by the garage doors, caught his attention and he crossed the snow-covered lawn at a dead run.

The bastard had hold of her by the arm and, Max realized with a jolt of pure rage, by the scarf wrapped around her neck.

"Let her go."

If he'd done as requested, Max might have resisted the primal impulse pounding through his veins. But Gregg didn't release his stranglehold grip on Diana until Max lifted him off the ground by the coat collar, and when he made the mistake of opening his spiteful little mouth, Max planted a fist in the center of that sneering insult. He would have liked to repeat the procedure, once for every time he'd bullied Diana and once for every insult. But the worm went down in a heap in the snow and he was smart enough not to get up again.

Max swallowed his disappointment and called the police.

This time Diana didn't argue with his decision to call the law or with his decision to stay the night. Max had expected both. All through the questioning and the charging procedure, he'd sensed her gathering her defences and preparing to shut him out. And when they were finally alone, when he said "I'm staying" in a brook-no-argument tone, she did open her mouth to protest.

He silenced that with a hard, possessive, I've-had-enough kiss that flared into instant passion. They'd made love with an urgent intensity that shattered any remaining doubts. She was his. He was staying. To-morrow they would work out what to do about all their future tomorrows.

He'd woken wanting her again, slowly this time with the night behind them and the morning light soft on her body. But when he loped an arm across the bed he came up with nothing but tangled sheets. From beyond the closed bathroom door came a low electrical hum and he squinted at his watch.

Seven-fifteen.

Later than he usually slept—he'd needed to catch up, to relax from yesterday's drama, to unwind the last coils of tension. But even if she insisted on going into work, as she'd intended before the Gregg incident exploded, it wasn't too late to entice her back where he wanted her.

He swung his legs over the side of the bed and

padded to the bathroom. When he pushed the door open, the hum escalated to a pitchy wail. Diana, drying her hair, the expression on her face abstracted. For a second he just drank in the perfect picture of his woman relaxed and unselfconscious, the way he wanted to find her every morning for the rest of his life.

Except preferably in his bed. Without the robe.

He may have moved, or breathed. Whatever caught her attention caught it quickly and she startled upright, her squeak of surprise silenced beneath the dryer's howl. Their eyes met in the mirror, hers as round as the O of her mouth, and he smiled his good morning.

She didn't, and Max realized that her surprised expression held traces of yesterday's scare. With a muffled oath at his own clumsiness, he closed down the space separating them and wrapped his arms around her waist. "I'm sorry," he murmured against her ear. "I didn't mean to frighten you."

For a minute she stood stiffly in his arms, her own stretched awkwardly in hairdrying position. When he attempted to take the sleek silver machine from her hand, he realized that a strand of hair had caught, tangled somehow in the air intake vent. Max took hold of the dryer and inspected the damage.

"Can you get it out?" she asked.

"I can try."

That was no hardship. He got to breathe the scent of her freshly washed skin, still warm and moist from her shower. He took his time and once he'd freed her, he lifted her onto the vanity.

"Stop." Her hand, planted in the middle of his chest

reinforced the crisp command. "I have to get ready for work."

"It's early yet."

"I want to go in early, to catch up."

"Okay." He was prepared to be reasonable. He was prepared to do whatever it took to wipe the remnant worry from her expression, to make her smile, to bring her gaze up from chin level to meet his eyes. "This won't have to take long."

She puffed out a sound that was a small part laughter but mostly exasperation. "Oh, please. You don't do anything in half measures."

Pleased to have earned that recognition, Max grinned. He planted a hand either side of her hips and leaned in to nuzzle the side of her neck. The restraining pressure of her palm against his chest increased until he leaned back.

"It wasn't a compliment," she said curtly. "We need to talk."

Of course they did. He'd just hoped for a little more time to show her they belonged together. He rested his face against hers for a second, cheek to cheek, while he attempted to shift focus. Being buck naked, his body's focus was blatantly obvious. "I don't suppose we could have this conversation back in bed?"

"No…although it might be more comfortable if we have it with clothes on."

If Max had been listening with his upper body, he'd have picked up the distancing vibes way back at *we need to talk.* Now he picked them up but he refused to be shut out. He eased back into his own space— barely—and waited for her to talk.

"What are you doing here, Max?" she asked without prevarication.

"You think I would leave you alone? After last night?"

"After last night, Gregg will not be back. You know you didn't have to stay."

"I didn't have to," he said simply. "I wanted to."

Her expression tightened, as if denying those words admission. "You said before we went to Kentucky that you would be going home as soon as your business was done."

"That's what I intended. But I don't have to rush right back."

"Maybe you don't have to hurry back, but you do need to go back at some point. I think it would be better if we acknowledged that fact and—"

"Better for whom?"

She blinked at his interruption. Moistened her lips before resetting them in a firm line. Max wanted to kiss that gravity away, but he settled for brushing his thumb across her bottom lip. With cupping her face in his hand so she couldn't look away.

"Come with me," he said with quiet intensity.

Their eyes met and held, hers bright with momentary hope. Or at least that's what he thought he saw before she shook her head. "To Australia? I can't just up and…" She blew out a choppy breath. "I can't."

Oh, but she could. Despite her resolute expression Max sensed a subtle yielding in the husky tone of her voice.

"Take some time off. Holiday time. Sick days."

She blinked and in the space of a heartbeat the resolve was back in her face, her posture, the hand she raised to stop his approach. Resolve and something else he couldn't identify. He was still trying to work out what he'd said when she pushed off the vanity and ducked past him. "I need to get ready for work."

He followed her into the bedroom, found her rifling through clothes with a kind of panicky desperation. He put a hand on her shoulder and felt her inner tension. His nature urged him to push, to demand an answer, to break down this wall while the foundations still shook with her indecision.

But instincts honed by these past days together, by the lessons learned in Kentucky, reined him back in. He had time for a little patience and he had another incentive that would mean more to Diana than words he wasn't sure he could deliver.

"Think about it." With restraint he leaned down and kissed her cheek. "We'll talk at lunch."

"Let me make sure I understand what you're saying…" Given that her brain remained punchdrunk from Max's come-with-me proclamation several hours before, Diana thought she may have misheard or misinterpreted her boss's words. "Nash Fortune wants to buy my collection?"

"Not the whole collection. A selection," Jeffrey stressed. He beamed like a proud parent. "I thought about having champagne on ice to celebrate your first commercial sale, but then I remembered the roses." He rolled his eyes and grimaced. "And I decided against."

Diana couldn't imagine the effect champagne in the morning would have on her wildly flailing emotions. At the moment she struggled to contain a whoop of delight.

Half an hour ago she'd battled the rough ache of tears in the back of her throat.

All because the words *come with me* had triggered exploding kernels of hope in her heart.

Oh, yes, she wanted to go with him—to Australia, to Timbuktu, to Mars—but *not* on an extended holiday fling. She wanted more than that and during the night, when she'd loved him with her heart and her soul wide open, when he'd kissed the fingerprint bruises on her arm with devastating tenderness and held her close to his heart, she had fooled herself into believing that he felt the same riptide of emotion.

The same wondrous sense of complete connection.

But, no. He wanted her to take holiday leave. If she'd been quick-witted enough, she would have asked "for how long?" Just so she knew what to pack! Instead she, who had suggested their need to talk in the first place, had bolted from further discussion before the threatening tears erupted. By lunch she may have gathered her defences and formulated an answer that didn't include *yes, Max.*

"Have we spaced out again?" Jeffrey cleared his throat loudly. And winked. "That must have been some weekend in Lexington!"

He knew about Max. From Eliza, of course, since she had called Jeffrey to pass on the message about Diana missing work yesterday. The notion of them talking about her private life caused an uncomfortable niggle in Diana's stomach. She despised gossip. And she hated the smutty subtext of Jeffey's wink. "I would prefer if we didn't discuss my private life," she said archly.

Jeffrey opened his mouth and shut it again, as if he'd

thought better of whatever he was about to say. "None of my business," he said finally. "Unless he's thinking of taking you back to Australia, in which case that does impact my business plans."

The business proposal. The roses, the trashed card. Otherwise occupied, Diana hadn't given them another thought in the five days since. This might just take her mind off Max.

"Can we talk about that now?" she asked, sitting up straighter in her chair.

"Absolutely." Jeffrey rubbed his hands together. "Where do I start?"

"He offered you a partnership in *Click?*" Max stopped slap-bang in the center of the sidewalk, the only sign that her revelation had knocked him off balance.

"I guess that is it," Diana confirmed. "In summary."

"You don't look very excited."

She supposed she should feel more jazzed, but Jeffrey's curveball had whizzed by her at the worst possible time. She was too distracted by the nagging voice in the back of her head recanting the proposal she *really* wanted to hear.

Come with me to Australia, Diana, not for a holiday, but forever.

"I will be excited," she said emphatically, talking over the top of that fanciful imp. "I just need some time to digest the details and the implications. Partnerships in my family have left me with some cause for circumspection."

"Your father's?" he guessed and she nodded.

"Not that I want to compare David's idea of a partnership deal with Jeffrey's."

From the corner of her eye she saw two women

looking back over their shoulders as they passed, and she realized they were partly blocking the pedestrian traffic. She should have waited until they were at the restaurant before telling him, but when he'd arrived to take her to lunch—earlier than she'd expected—he'd asked the leading question, "How was your morning?" and she just blurted out the news.

Now she resumed walking. "Where are we going for lunch?"

Did she imagine his hesitation? "I bought the makings of a picnic. I thought we could take a drive up to the Falls. It'll be easier to talk without interruption."

True. Except it was February. "It's not exactly picnic weather," she pointed out.

Paused at the passenger side of the Lexus, he studied her face for a moment. Perhaps her nose was turning blue in the icy wind because he said, "Then let's go to your house…if that's all right with you?"

She nodded, appreciating the fact that he'd bothered to ask. "Let's do that. It will be easier to talk if my teeth aren't chattering."

A woman she recognized as a recent gallery client gave them a long sideways look as she passed. Max doffed his hat and the woman smiled at them both before hurrying off. "Does everyone in this town read that bloody column?" he asked.

Diana frowned. "What column?"

His gaze met hers after the briefest hesitation, and Diana felt a sinking weight in the pit of her stomach. "I gather you haven't seen the gossip page in today's newspaper then?"

Ten

This was not going as Max had planned. First she'd dropped the bombshell about Jeffrey's partnership proposal. Now he had to show her the gossip column. He hoped like hell she had a long lunch break or all his morning's rushed preparations would be in vain.

Glancing across the car's center console at Diana's face, he couldn't tell if she was truly unmoved or doing a mighty fine job of disguising her emotions. Once they had gotten into his car, he had opened the paper straight to the society pages, to the short column of gossipy pieces about local identities, with no names named.

This week's lead item didn't need any names.

She started to read it out loud, her voice as clear as the midday February sky, as crisp as the air whipping off the snow.

"Which snap-happy local gallery assistant and which hunky Australian cousin to Sioux Falls' most powerful family are reported to have spent the last weekend in a luxury Kentucky hotel suite? It might have been snowing outside but we hear things between this gorgeous couple are hot and heavy…and not for the first time."

She paused, as if to consider this line, and when she resumed reading there was a different quality to her voice, a choked thickness that could have been due to outraged anger or to intense disillusionment.

"Our source tells us they were once young lovebirds but our local beauty chose marriage to a wealthy Hollywood producer. Some girls get all the luck—especially when they're the daughter of Broadway stage royalty."

Her voice trailed off but Max knew she'd read silently on to the end.

"At least this explains some things," she said evenly.

"What things?"

"Oh, things such as the number of people who popped in to the gallery this morning 'just to have a look around.' The odd comments, the curious looks. I kept checking to see if I had smudged toner on my face." Her small smile held not a grain of humor. "I guess I can kiss Diana Young goodbye. I am now officially Diana Fielding again."

"Is that so bad?" Braking at an intersection, he shot her an assessing look. "You told me once that it's only a name. You said you were the same person."

"Diana Young is a name. Diana Fielding is, I quote, *the daughter of Broadway stage royalty.*"

Okay, so she didn't like the notoriety or the label, but he sensed that wasn't the only thing lining her forehead with worry. He only had to wait another half-block before he discovered what else bothered her about the piece.

"All my life I've been the good girl, the boringly sensible sister in a family of artistic and rebellious spirits. Until I married so quickly and so young, the scandal sheets couldn't find a single interesting thing to write about me. I move to Sioux Falls to escape all that and *this* happens!"

"It doesn't say anything that's not the truth," Max pointed out. "We're both unattached. It isn't hurting our families. Do you think it's worth fretting over?"

"That's not the point," she countered in a rush. "It happened out of state and I didn't tell anyone I was going. They shouldn't have even known about you and me going to Lexington, let alone printing the news!"

Still several blocks from her house, he pulled over and killed the engine. The last notes of her indignation still steamed through the vehicle. *I didn't tell anyone. They shouldn't have even known.*

Eyes narrowed, Max turned to face her. "Is there any reason you were so set on keeping this a secret?"

"Because I don't like being stared at. I don't like being a curiosity. I don't want people talking about my private business. And I *hate* that I'm going to go to sleep tonight worrying over how this got in the paper." She lifted her hands in entreaty. "The only person I spoke to from Kentucky was Eliza. She wouldn't tell a columnist knowingly, but now I wonder if she told someone who told someone. I can't think of any other primary source."

"Case has a theory."

"I didn't know he was back from his honeymoon. You spoke to him this morning?"

"I went around to his office after I left your house. He showed me the paper—" he gestured at the copy she'd let slip to the floor "—and he suggested that the 'source' might be someone on the Fortune's staff."

"At Dakota Fortune?"

"At the estate, on the household staff. Apparently Nash's second wife…Tina, is it?"

"Trina Watters. Blake and Skylar's mother."

Max nodded, confirming the woman's identity. "According to Case she has a way of finding out snippets of information she shouldn't have access to. This same column hinted at Case's engagement plans before he'd popped the question to Gina. That's when he started suspecting someone on the staff of eavesdropping on conversations and picking up phone extensions."

"Spying for Trina?"

He shrugged. "I don't know if it's true and Case has no proof."

"From what I've heard of Trina, it's possible. And I suppose someone could have picked up an extension when I was talking to Eliza or when she called Jeffrey to pass on my message. It makes more sense than anything I can think of."

They sat in silent contemplation, the jeweler's box a heavy presence in his pocket since she'd asked about his visit to Case's office. Short on time, he'd needed his cousin's local knowledge and recommendation. With everything else going on today, the timing sucked but he didn't want her retreating again. He didn't want her thinking about the partnership and every other reason she had to stay in Sioux Falls.

He had no intention of leaving without her and he had to up the ante.

The possibility of rejection made him antsy, the need to get this over and done with prickled like an impatient itch in his spine. He could start the car, take her home as they'd agreed downtown, but that would give her the advantage of home territory. He liked it better here, the location neutral, the perimeter enclosed. She couldn't walk away. The advantage was his.

"We need to finish that talk."

"Yes, we do." She drew an audible breath, as if sucking up purpose or courage or strength, but her eyes remained fixed on her lap where she folded her hands in carefully staged composure. "I can't come to Australia, Max."

"Because of that partnership proposal?"

She looked up sharply, alerted by the disparaging tone of his question. "Is there something I should know about Jeffrey's offer? Something I don't know?"

"Have you considered that it may be more than a business partnership?"

"We are friends, we are business colleagues. That's all."

"Maybe that's true. Or maybe he's been circling, nice and patient, waiting for the right time to move in."

"No." She shook her head, discounting that option without hesitation. "You're wrong."

"You don't think the timing of this offer is significant? You don't think he saw me cutting in with the gifts last week? That he's had to signal his intentions by offering you a bigger prize?"

"Is that how you see me? As a prize to be won? Because if that is the case," she said slowly, each word enunciated with chillingly clear enunciation, "it would appear that you won the big prize last weekend."

"Now hang on, Diana." Max raised his hands, intent on halting that train of thought. "I was attempting to point out the suspect timing of this proposal. Your boss wants to tie you to his business, with a legal partnership and with your capital, right at a time when you might be contemplating leaving. To me that smacks of the very kind of manipulation you would want to avoid in business, given the family background you mentioned downtown."

Color flushed her skin and her eyes glimmered with what looked like rising indignation. "Three things. Firstly—" she held up her index finger "—Jeffrey was going to make the offer last week until I cancelled the dinner meeting on Wednesday night. He knew nothing about you, in my past or my present, that might have instigated his offer at that point. Secondly—" she ticked that off with her middle finger "—I don't accept your reason for his proposal. I know I'm a good photographer. I know I will make a valuable partner."

It sounded as though that was a done deal. Icy disquiet flickered through Max's skin as he asked, "The third thing?"

She raised a third digit. "And why might I be contemplating leaving Sioux Falls? To go on an extended holiday to the other side of the world? To give up everything I've fought so hard to establish for myself? My home and my life and the first rewarding job I've had in my whole life…and for what? What exactly are you offering me, Max?"

"Whatever it takes, Diana."

Her chin came up, unimpressed. Her eyes glittered with something that may have been pride and may have been anger. "Whatever it takes to close the deal? To get what you want? Is that what you mean, Max?"

"Whatever it takes to prove that we belong together. Commitment, a proposal, a ring." He counted those off with his fingers, clear and concise, so there was no misunderstanding. "All the things you told me you wanted last time, Diana, before you walked away without giving me a chance to consider. That's *my* partnership proposal."

For a long moment their gazes clashed, the connection fraught with the magnitude of his offer. Max held himself rigid, unable to embellish, unprepared to beg, incapable of putting out any more. When he'd gone to see Case, when he'd told him of his plans, when he'd shaken his hand and accepted his best wishes along with a jeweler's recommendation, conviction had coursed through his veins and firmed the set of his jaw and the strength of his handshake.

He'd known he wanted this.

Now, with the initial burst of shocked hope dimming to wariness in her grey-green eyes, his certainty nosedived. Even before she moistened her lips, while she studied her folded hands and straightened the pleats of her skirt in a gesture of nerves and uncertainty, he knew that he was about to drive away with a pair of airline tickets and an unwanted diamond ring in his pocket.

Exactly the same as the last time.

"I'm sorry, Max," she said, and the pained expression in the eyes she turned to meet his almost convinced him that she really was sorry. "That's just not enough."

"What else can I offer? What the hell else do you want?"

"To be loved." Tears shimmered briefly in her eyes before she looked away, but he heard the rough edge of that moisture in her voice when she continued. "That's all I ever wanted from you."

He stared at her, perplexed. "What do you think I'm offering? Weren't you listening?"

"I heard your words. I heard your offer. I just don't believe the reason behind it."

His stark one-word oath cut through the cold interior of the vehicle and she lifted her hands to rub at her arms. Max knew that feeling, that bone-deep cold of frustrated hopes. He could feel it frosting his own veins and setting hard and tight in his gut. "You want reasons? How about this last weekend? How about last night? How about those marks on your arm and the fact that you need a keeper to protect you from—"

"I don't need you for that, Max."

"What do you need me for, Diana? Sex? Another dirty weekender out of town that you'd prefer to keep secret from your friends?"

Her eyes widened to dark pools of shock in her pale face. "That's not true. That is not—"

"No? You talk about what you want from me, about

my reasons. Maybe you need to examine yours, Diana. Maybe it's time to be honest with yourself about what you really want."

She didn't answer and he felt the crippling blow of that silence strike midchest. He was right. She had no answer because he'd called it right.

She *had* only relented and slept with him because it was out of town. No one would even have known about their extended one-night stand but for the newspaper column. She'd returned to Sioux Falls expecting to kiss him goodbye, until Gregg Young's reappearance and the gossip piece and his unwanted proposal complicated matters.

Removing one of those complications was easy. He reached for the ignition and turned on the engine. "I'll take you back to work," he said coldly. "I assume that's what you think you want."

Yes, she'd lied, *that is what I want.* The only other place she could have asked him to take her was home, and after the events of the past week her home was no longer a comforting haven. Like her arms it bore the tainted bruises of Gregg's intrusion.

Like her heart it bore the bruising imprint of Max.

Kitchen, sunroom, living room. The guestroom and her own bedroom and bath. Everywhere held a memory, the flash of his smile, a raw lick of his heat, his sleep-tousled head on her pillow.

His proposal of all she'd ever wanted, if only the gift had come wrapped in his love.

All afternoon and through the long, restless night

she'd held her shattered emotions together with the fire of righteous anger. How could she love a man who equated a marriage proposal with a business contest, who saw her as a prize to be won? A man who, when it looked like he was losing, turned the argument around by accusing her of not knowing what she wanted?

She knew. She'd told him as much. He chose not to listen.

And that left her to consider her other choices, starting with Jeffrey's expansion plans. It didn't matter what Max thought about her boss's motivation in proposing a partnership. *She* knew the offer was sincere. *She* knew she had talent and that she wanted to make a career out of photography.

What she hadn't yet decided was whether she wanted to start that career as a partner in *Click*.

That still occupied her mind as she drove out to the Fortune Estate the next morning. Thinking about the business kept her from dwelling on the two items in her coat pocket, two items she'd chosen to return in person…or as close as her courage would allow her to in person.

One was a check she intended handing back to Nash Fortune.

The other was the prettiest charm bracelet she had ever seen.

In the five minutes she'd stood in the foyer of the Fortune's home, waiting for the housekeeper to return with Nash Fortune, Diana had rattled through a ten-month collection of emotions. Impatience, fear, dogged determination, annoyance, fear, worry, dread, fear, and two dozen others too confusing and complex and maddening to label.

Right now, as she listened to the sound of approaching footsteps, she would have chosen any one of them over her present state of jittery, heart-jumping nerves. She knew it was Max striding down the gallery. The confident cadence of the footfalls, the syncopated thump of her heart, the cold sweat in the palms of her hands.

When Nash Fortune came into view, she did a double take of surprise and, perversely, disappointment. Luckily he seemed lost in his own private worries, his shoulders slumped forward, his dark brows knit in a frown, and didn't notice her until after she'd reassembled her poise.

"Diana. What can I do for you?"

"I want to talk to you about the photos you bought. From the gallery. *Click*," she added when he showed no sign of recognition.

"Ah, yes. Of course." He smiled then, and she realized that he'd been distracted and lost in his frown-inducing thoughts. "Come through, we'll have coffee."

"No, thank you, Mr. Fortune. I only called in to thank you, personally, for choosing my work. I am honored to think that my photos may be hung somewhere in this fabulous home." She reached into her pocket and withdrew the check. "Also, I wanted to return this."

For a second he gazed blankly at the slip of paper. "What's this, Diana?"

"It's your check, sir. I know you agreed to a sum with Jeffrey, but I don't feel comfortable accepting your money. I was very grateful for the chance to take the pictures of the estate and Sky's horses. I had intended giving the whole collection to your family when the exhibit ended, as a sign of that gratitude."

"I'm sure they will love to have them," he said, still ignoring the check.

"Please. Will you take the payment back?"

"No," he said after a moment's deliberation. "I appreciate your gesture and I understand why you are making it, Diana. But that check is fair payment for your talent in producing such outstanding images."

She acknowledged the compliment with a dip of her head. "In that case, I hope you don't mind if I donate the money, in your name, to the Children's Center charity fund." The return of his frown gave her pause. "Unless there is another charity you would prefer…?"

"I can't allow you to donate in my name," he said after a beat of hesitation. "That wouldn't be right."

"It's your check. Of course it's right."

"It's my check," he said slowly, "but it's not my money. It's Max's."

Unprepared for the mention of his name, Diana's heart crashed hard. Then it resumed its beat in time with the clank of the puzzle pieces coming together. "You bought the pictures on Max's behalf?"

Another attempt to impress her, no doubt, and she wondered when he'd planned on springing this surprise ploy. After she'd agreed to his no-love proposal? Or did he intend using this as a last ditch means of proving his affection?

The manipulative hound.

"I see," she said evenly to Nash. "Do you happen to know where I can find him?"

Diana left the house mad—so mad she decided to tramp the long curving drive to the stable block in an attempt to cool down. She didn't want to fire another round of bitter hurting accusations. For once she wanted an honest discussion with direct answers.

With every icy scrunch of her boots another question fired through her mind. By the time she strode through the arched entryway of the central barn, a dozen different points lay poised for delivery. She didn't pause to look around or ask directions this time. She sensed she would find him where she'd found him the first time.

This time she didn't need to remember her mother's lessons in poise and presence. Her insides trembled up a storm but her stride remained confident and certain. She knew what she wanted and she was in exactly the right frame of mind to let Max know.

She had just turned the corner of the U-shaped alleyway, when he came out of the second to last stable. He took a few seconds to close the door behind him and then to rub a big hand down the face and under the jaw of the Kentucky beauty inside. He wore the cowboy's suede jacket and a hat dipped low on his forehead, and Diana's heart responded with the same sweet abandon as the first time she'd watched him crooning to this beautiful horse.

The same as it had always done and would always do.

"Hello, Max."

Two simple words, yet they ached with the misery

of loving him and knowing that would never be enough without proof that he felt the same.

He looked up, his expression flat and unsmiling, but from the shadow of his wide-brimmed she caught the gleam of green fire. Surprise, yes, and more. "Diana. What are you doing here?"

"I drove out to return a check to Nash. He used it to pay for photographs but he says the money isn't his."

She walked forward and held it out, a fluttering testimonial to the truth.

"Why are you returning it?" he asked.

"I can't take money for those photos. They were not for sale."

"You want them back?"

A question rather than the truthful straight-out answers she sought, but at least he hadn't denied knowledge. The check was Nash's so he could have done so.

"That depends," she said in answer to his question.

"On?"

"Your reason for acquiring them in such an underhanded fashion."

His gaze narrowed in response to that pejorative description and Diana gave herself a swift mental kick. Nice job in keeping the discussion cool and unaccusatory. "That day I came to the gallery and expressed interest in your pictures, you told me I couldn't buy them."

"I doubted your motives."

"You do a lot of that."

She sucked in a breath and counted to five. That was just enough time to cool the instant denial on her tongue. Instead she nodded. "Yes, but I believe I've had just cause.

Your gifts were an attempt to get me into bed. I thought your interest in my pictures was more of the same."

"There you go. You wouldn't trust that I might just want them, no strings attached."

"Why did you want them?" she countered. "Because you like the images or because I took them?"

"Both, okay? I came to your gallery that day because you invited me to."

Diana frowned.

"The day we had coffee, the first day it snowed. You told me I should come and check out your work, to ensure you knew your job."

"And you liked them enough to buy some?"

"Yes, but I also wanted them because they were yours. If you don't like that—" Max shrugged "—then, too bad."

"Because they're mine," she echoed.

"At least I had some part of you to take back home. Something of you to love."

Her eyes widened on that last word, then narrowed. "Love?"

That scornful note burrowed right under his skin and scraped every raw exposed nerve. "Yes, I said love. That's what I offered you when I asked you to come home to Australia with me. That's what—"

"You didn't mention love," she cut in, her cheeks colored with the same rising fervor he heard in her voice. "You mentioned wanting and that is something totally different. You don't love me, Max. You never have."

The accusation flayed the last of his patience, the last of his pride. "If I never loved you, then why did I come after you?"

"You've never come after me. Not once. Unless you count your attempts to bed me. I'm the one who came looking—"

"I don't mean now. I mean ten years ago."

"What are you saying?"

Their gazes locked, hers wide and bright with confusion. What the hell, Max thought. If she wanted proof of his love, of his commitment, then what more could he offer? "I came to New York the day of your wedding. I was there, Diana."

"I don't understand...."

"I came to America to find you, to talk you into coming home. I found out the address from a maid at your father's Manhattan apartment and I drove out to the Hamptons. I wanted proof, too, you see. Proof that you were marrying another man instead of me."

She shook her head in slow disbelief. "You were there...and you didn't do anything?"

"You walked into that garden on your father's arm wearing a white dress. What did you expect me to do?"

"If you loved me, then why did you let me marry him?"

"Because I imagined you *wanted* to marry him, Diana. What else would a man think when confronted with that scenario?"

Wired with all the pain of that discovery, his words cut through the cavernous silence of the barn and shimmered in her eyes.

"Why didn't you say anything?" she asked thickly.

"What do you suppose I could have said? 'Congratulations'?"

"I meant now. I meant the other day. I meant any

time. Oh, Max." She lifted an unsteady hand, the one still holding the check, and dashed at the tears brimming from her eyes. "I didn't know."

Those last anguished words, the expression on her face, the tentative step she took toward him....

Max's heart checked out for a beat. "Didn't know what?"

"You told me you almost married someone once. That was me, wasn't it? You came out here to marry me, even though you'd said you weren't ready for that commitment."

"I wanted you in my life, whatever it took."

She nodded. Then made another futile attempt to stop the flow of tears. "Are you going to tell me why?"

The warm flood of hope stilled in his veins. "Curse it, Diana, I've just shown what you meant to me. I've laid myself bare. What more proof can you ask of me?"

"I don't want proof, Max. I want to hear the words."

"I love you? That's all?"

She smiled through the tears. "That's all I've ever wanted, Max."

"What about the partnership? What about *Click?*"

"I decided on my way out here that I'm not taking it. I don't want to be a partner in anything that isn't mine, that isn't here—" she touched a hand to her chest "—in my heart and my soul."

"I thought that's what photography was to you."

"It is and will always be, but it's not my yacht."

The tears were streaming freely now, and she gave up her attempts to staunch them. They were happy tears, tears of the sun and of the heart and of her future. He hadn't yet said the words but they were there, in the hint of a grin and the understanding in his eyes.

He knew what she was saying.

The yacht was *their* dream, the symbol of whatever they built together.

"Are you sure this is what you want?" he asked.

She lifted her hand, soggy check and all, and touched his cheek. "*This* is what I want."

He kissed her then, with a thoroughness that curled her toes and a tenderness that curled around her heart. And when he'd finished kissing her breathless, he lifted her by the waist and swung her around until she laughed out loud with giddy joy. And as he eased her back to her feet in a long, delicious slide down his body, she heard the teeniest clink of charms as the bracelet settled back into the corner of her coat pocket after the wild ride.

Later she would wear it, possibly with little else.

Later, when she was back in his bed.

But now she wanted to hear the words, this time with the proper reverence, this time with all the emotion he'd unfurled in her heart. "Tell me," she said, her voice barely more than a whisper. "Tell me and then ask me all over again."

He chuckled at the request but he didn't have to ask her to explain. First he took the ruined check from her hand and tossed it away. A sign of how little money would matter in their future, she decided.

Without hesitation he went down on one knee, her hand gripped in his. And there, on the aged cobblestones before the witnessing eyes of the horse she called Maggie, he turned the first of her dreams into reality.

"I love you, Diana." The intensity in his voice and in the forest-green depths of his eyes was a conduit straight to the core of her soul. "Will you come with me to Australia? Will you take my name and become part of my family? Will you be the heart of my life?"

"Yes." She sunk down to meet him. "Yes," she whispered against his lips. "And yes," she breathed into his kiss, and Maggie whinnied her approval.

* * * * *

Don't miss the next book in the
DAKOTA FORTUNES series.
Be sure to pick up
FORTUNE'S VENGEFUL GROOM
by Charlene Sands,
available in March.

Happily ever after is just the beginning...

Turn the page for a sneak preview of
A HEARTBEAT AWAY
by
Eleanor Jones

Harlequin Everlasting—Every great love
has a story to tell. ™
A brand-new series from Harlequin Books

Special? A prickle ran down my neck and my heart started to beat in my ears. Was today really special?

"Tuck in," he ordered.

I turned my attention to the feast that he had spread out on the ground. Thick, home-cooked-ham sandwiches, sausage rolls fresh from the oven and a huge variety of mouthwatering scones and pastries. Hunger pangs took over, and I closed my eyes and bit into soft homemade bread.

When we were finally finished, I lay back against the bluebells with a groan, clutching my stomach.

Daniel laughed. "Your eyes are bigger than your stomach," he told me.

I leaned across to deliver a punch to his arm, but he rolled away, and when my fist met fresh air I collapsed in a fit of giggles before relaxing on my back and staring up into the flawless blue sky. We lay like that for quite a while, Daniel and I, side by side in companionable silence, until he stretched out his hand in an arc that encompassed the whole area.

"Don't you think that this is the most beautiful place in the entire world?"

His voice held a passion that echoed my own feelings, and I rose onto my elbow and picked a buttercup to hide the emotion that clogged my throat.

"Roll over onto your back," I urged, prodding him with my forefinger. He obliged with a broad grin, and I reached across to place the yellow flower beneath his chin.

"Now, let us see if you like butter."

When a yellow light shone on the tanned skin below his jaw, I laughed.

"There…you do."

For an instant our eyes met, and I had the strangest sense that I was drowning in those honey-brown depths. The scent of bluebells engulfed me. A roaring filled my ears, and then, unexpectedly, in one smooth movement Daniel rolled me onto my back and plucked a buttercup of his own.

"And do *you* like butter, Lucy McTavish?" he asked. When he placed the flower against my skin, time stood still.

His long lean body was suspended over mine, pinning me against the grass. Daniel…dear, comfortable, familiar Daniel was suddenly bringing out in me the strangest sensations.

"Do you, Lucy McTavish?" he asked again, his voice low and vibrant.

My eyes flickered toward his, the whisper of a sigh escaped my lips and although a strange lethargy had crept into my limbs, I somehow felt as if all my nerve endings were on fire. He felt it, too—I could see it in his warm brown eyes. And when he lowered his face to mine, it seemed to me the most natural thing in the world.

None of the kisses I had ever experienced could have even begun to prepare me for the feel of Daniel's lips on mine. My entire body floated on a tide of ecstasy that shut out everything but his soft, warm mouth, and I knew that this was what I had been waiting for the whole of my life.

"Oh, Lucy." He pulled away to look into my eyes. "Why haven't we done this before?"

Holding his gaze, I gently touched his cheek, then I curled my fingers through the short thick hair at the base of his skull, overwhelmed by the longing to drown again in the sensations that flooded our bodies. And when his long tanned fingers crept across my tingling skin, I knew I could deny him nothing.

* * * * *

Be sure to look for
A HEARTBEAT AWAY,
available February 27, 2007.

And look, too, for THE DEPTH OF LOVE
by Margot Early, the story of a couple
who must learn that love comes
in many guises—and in the end
it's the only thing that counts.

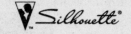

Silhouette® Desire

Millionaire of the Month

Bound by the terms of a will,
six wealthy bachelors discover
the ultimate inheritance.

USA TODAY bestselling author

MAUREEN CHILD

Millionaire of the Month: **Nathan Barrister**
Source of Fortune: **Hotel empire**
Dominant Personality Trait: **Gets what he wants**

THIRTY DAY AFFAIR
SD #1785 Available in March

When Nathan Barrister arrives at the Lake Tahoe
lodge, all he can think about is how soon he can
leave. His one-month commitment feels like solitary
confinement—until a snowstorm traps him with lovely
Keira Sanders. Suddenly a thirty-day affair sounds like
just the thing to pass the time…

In April,
#1791 HIS FORBIDDEN FIANCÉE, Christie Ridgway

In May,
#1797 BOUND BY THE BABY, Susan Crosby

Hearts racing
Blood pumping
Pulses accelerating

Falling in love can be a blur...especially at **180 mph!**

So if you crave the thrill of the chase—on and off the track—you'll love

SPEED DATING
by Nancy Warren!

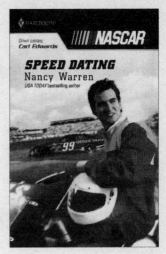

Hearts racing
Blood pumping
Pulses accelerating

Falling in love can be
a blur…especially at
180 mph!

So if you crave the thrill
of the chase—on and off
the track—you'll love

SPEED DATING
by **Nancy Warren!**

REQUEST YOUR FREE BOOKS!

2 FREE NOVELS PLUS 2 FREE GIFTS!

Silhouette® Desire®

Passionate, Powerful, Provocative!

YES! Please send me 2 FREE Silhouette Desire® novels and my 2 FREE gifts. After receiving them, if I don't wish to receive any more books, I can return the shipping statement marked "cancel." If I don't cancel, I will receive 6 brand-new novels every month and be billed just $3.80 per book in the U.S., or $4.47 per book in Canada, plus 25¢ shipping and handling per book and applicable taxes, if any*. That's a savings of almost 15% off the cover price! I understand that accepting the 2 free books and gifts places me under no obligation to buy anything. I can always return a shipment and cancel at any time. Even if I never buy another book from Silhouette, the two free books and gifts are mine to keep forever.

225 SDN EEXJ 326 SDN EEXU

Name _____ (PLEASE PRINT)

Address _____ Apt. _____

City _____ State/Prov. _____ Zip/Postal Code _____

Signature (if under 18, a parent or guardian must sign)

Mail to the **Silhouette Reader Service™:**
IN U.S.A.: P.O. Box 1867, Buffalo, NY 14240-1867
IN CANADA: P.O. Box 609, Fort Erie, Ontario L2A 5X3

Not valid to current Silhouette Desire subscribers.

Want to try two free books from another line?
Call 1-800-873-8635 or visit www.morefreebooks.com.

* Terms and prices subject to change without notice. NY residents add applicable sales tax. Canadian residents will be charged applicable provincial taxes and GST. This offer is limited to one order per household. All orders subject to approval. Credit or debit balances in a customer's account(s) may be offset by any other outstanding balance owed by or to the customer. Please allow 4 to 6 weeks for delivery.

Your Privacy: Silhouette is committed to protecting your privacy. Our Privacy Policy is available online at www.eHarlequin.com or upon request from the Reader Service. From time to time we make our lists of customers available to reputable firms who may have a product or service of interest to you. If you would prefer we not share your name and address, please check here. ☐

SDES07

This February...

Silhouette®

Romantic

SUSPENSE

Excitement, danger and passion guaranteed!

Same great authors and riveting editorial
you've come to know and love
from Silhouette Intimate Moments.

> *New York Times*
> bestselling author
> Beverly Barton
> is back with the
> latest installment
> in her popular
> miniseries,
> The Protectors.
> HIS ONLY
> OBSESSION
> is available
> next month from
> Silhouette®
> Romantic Suspense

Look for it wherever you buy books!

From reader-favorite

MARGARET WAY

Cattle Rancher, Convenient Wife

On sale March 2007.

**"Margaret Way delivers…
vividly written, dramatic stories."**
—*Romantic Times BOOKreviews*

*For more wonderful wedding stories,
watch for Patricia Thayer's new miniseries
starting in April 2007.*